RACHAEL'S JAUNT

JOANNE AUSTEN BROWN

RACHAEL'S JAUNT

JOANNE AUSTEN BROWN

Book One ~ Come With Me

Title: Rachael's Jaunt

Copyright © 2020 Joanne Austen Brown

BOOKS BY JOANNE AUSTEN BROWN

Always Louisa ~ Book One: Always Series

We all have friends and family who encourage us. I had a dear friend who passed away just recently who loved my work. She would love me telling her of my characters and my plots.

We met regularly for breakfast and on other occasions. We would talk, often for hours. To me she was a friend, a mentor, and a beautiful human being. Martha, I miss you more than you will ever know.

Rest in peace, my dearest friend.

FAIRY HILL, ABERLOUR, SCOTLAND

"You know, they don't understand about our hills." Drake wandered to the edge and looked down at the sleeping village. The faint teal-blue light surrounding him. The world was quiet.

"I appreciate what you say but they will have to learn that we are responsible for all our hills. Once they did not doubt us. They will again believe in what we are capable of doing." Queen Alvina came to stand next to her consort. Her flowing dark blue gown glowed with the same teal blue light.

Drake continued. "I'm just not sure this is the way to do it. They do not believe in us or our magic anymore. Science now occupy people's minds. Not magic. So how can we expect them to respect our properties?"

She crossed her arms and gazed into his questioning eyes. "They'll have to learn to respect us again. Others in the past have. They will have to be reminded that we have been here longer than them and that we are part of this world too. I am sick and tired of waiting for them to realise the magic is still here. We must make a stand. If we do not do it now, we will be stuck in the world of the Fae and never come back here again. Do you want that?"

Drake bowed his head and closed his eyes. "But taking the girl could be damaging to us in the long run. People will think something terrible happened here."

He lifted his head to look at her and she knew he was just making sure they were doing the ethical thing.

Ethics be damned.

The fae had their rights too. "We both have looked at her history and her destiny and she is well suited to Duncan. He is her lost love after all. She will only be in the past for a short time. And one of our own will be watching out for her. Here, time will stand still while things take place in the past."

The two teal blue glowing figures moved slowly away from the edge of the hill. The light around them seemed to pulsate in the dark of the night. Their power would be evident if anyone could see.

"I know you're right. But I must ask the questions. What sort of consort would I be if I don't keep you on your toes?"

She placed her hand on his shoulder and he placed his around her waist. "I don't want to lose this place and Rachael is the only one who can save it for us. She will help this new world that exists to believe in magic again."

"You're right. It will be nice to be able to wander these hills again without being cautious about being seen. You do remember that this is where we met?"

"Of course. That is partly why I want to save it."

"I understand."

He looked deep into her eyes as he continued.

"But we now need to leave. Rachael is making her way up the hill."

The teal blue glow that had surrounded the figures gently faded and the figures were no longer there.

A figure got up from behind the rock in the centre of the hill and ran over to the bushes at its edge and got down onto the ground.

FAIRY HILL

A berlour, Scotland 2018

"Where are you?"

"I'm on a special mountain and I am sitting on a big rock, looking around me. The mountains, the river Spey. It's all so beautiful. I don't understand why it took me so long to come back here." The sun was just beginning to light the early morning sky giving everything a silver-grey appearance. Rachael Fielding breathed in the delicious scent of freshly mown grass as the early birds were singing their wake-up song.

"Do you really think you're doing the right thing? Wait a minute, what do you mean, *your* mountain? Rachael, what have you done?"

Samantha Cooper, her PA at the firm where she was a lawyer, as well as her best friend did not sound happy.

"Relax, I said a special mountain. Besides it's not a big mountain, more like a big hill. Where I come from it's flat, remember? For me, anything bigger than an ant hill is a mountain."

"Ok… Good… I can't understand why you just can't write at your farm here in Dubbo. Countryside is countryside." Her American accent was crisp and clear. Sam had only ever lived in her hometown Warwick in Rhode Island and now in Dubbo, Australia. She had no idea what a Scottish countryside was like.

Sam continued muttering in her ear as Rachael looked down to the dark silver-grey river Spey meandering gently through the dark green bracken laden hills that hugged the river to their base. A sense of peace descended onto her.

Sam's tirade continued, about the benefits of writing in a place that was familiar and comforting. How Rachael was making a mistake at not being at her desk with her cat 'Darnit' jumping all over her keyboard. Sam had even inspired the naming of her cat when the shy grey fluff ball was found wandering around the farm. Every time Sam got cross, she would say 'darn it' instead of swearing. Rachael loved that.

Her friend questioning her sanity and restlessness was what she had expected, but she had had enough now.

"Sam, stop, please. I am asking nicely, please. Can you see me smiling?"

"Stop being sarcastic. Rachael, I'm your friend and I worry about you. You know I personally would love to rip Josh's heart out of his chest, and I know you must get on with your life. Can't you just forget him and come home?"

Rachael shifted uncomfortably on the rock. "I've been spending so much time on work and my writing that I feel like I need to stop and take stock. I need this time away. It's not just Josh. He's gone and has been for ages, and I'm glad. But he keeps trying to get back into my life. So, I want this break somewhere far away. Especially after my parents…"

"But why Scotland? Why are you running away?"

Rachael sighed, then took a deep breath. She got off the rock and wandered around the top of the hill. Trust Sam to ask the tough questions.

"I'm not running away. But I can't see him coming after me here. He hasn't got access to my money anymore. I'm taking a break and that is exactly what I think, a break. Scotland is great and although Josh is the basis of every villain in all my books, I want to get rid of him once and for all." Rachael said. Who was she trying to convince? Sam or herself? "Please understand that I need this time, Sam. Scotland will soothe me. I can rid Josh from my books and my life completely. Don't tell him where I am, please?"

"I would never do that to you. He won't find out where you are from me."

"I'm sorry, Sam. I know you won't tell. I just need to relax. But I promise you that once I get my mojo back, I'll have some great stories for you to read. Maybe a whole new series."

She wanted to live in Scotland for a year to see if being here could bring her back the joy of writing she had lost. She had obtained the leave from her bosses but still had not told her friend of her lengthy plan.

"Scotsmen are hot I'll grant you that, but you will have to come up with something truly unique. Do you think you can come up with a series? Do you have a plot outline for the first book already? No. Don't answer that."

Rachael smiled.

"Okay Rach, go find a Scotsman who can heal that beautiful heart. I'll get off your back. But on one condition?"

"What's that?"

"Don't you dare buy a mountain!"

"Bye Sam. Look after Darnit, please?"

"No mountains. Okay?'

Rachael pressed the off on her phone and smiled. She went back to the rock and sat down, looking out over the valley and down to the village of Aberlour.

An occasional light flickered from house windows. The dawn sun was slowly rising. The River Spey was a dark silver snake like figure, in the middle of the valley. The last time she had been here, was on a trip through Scotland with her parents when she was only fifteen. She had no desire to go but once she had set foot on Scottish soil, she had fallen in love. The scenery, the people and most of all the history. Something wonderful had blossomed in her heart and never left her. And especially this little village. And now all these years later those first feelings flew back into her heart again.

She leant down and placed the phone in the pocket of her backpack. Her smile returned, as she searched over the landscape. The bird's early morning chatter and chirping was getting more intense. Watching the sky lighten had gladdened her heart. The air, crisp and clear. The grass and bracken were still green, but some areas of bracken were beginning to show hints of brown and the frosts that would come. Even in the dim light she could see it. Winter was not far away.

She lay back on the rock and looked up into the clearing night sky. Her thoughts became clearer too. Josh had to die, at least in her books, so that she could start again and perhaps find her real soul mate. She wasn't getting any younger and had already wasted too many years. Twenty-nine wasn't old but she could hear the ticking of her body clock and it was getting louder every year that passed. For the millionth time she asked herself if children were a part of her future or not. Would she remain a lawyer, even a writer? She didn't need a man. She was fine on her own, but it would be nice to have one.

FAIRY HILL

Aberlour Scotland – Tuesday 30*th* July 1822

"I'm just not sure the king is serious about his trip to Edinburgh. The Parliament want him away from the capital. They have their own agenda." Duncan Murray looked into Alasdair's laughing eyes. "And you don't need to look at me with jest either. We have been under the thumb of the English King for long enough. We are no longer Scotsman! It is all I can endure. We are being mocked, yet again." His anger met with another smile.

"Now Duncan, calm yourself, we have no choice. The king has requested all the lairds be present when he arrives in Edinburgh. If you do not attend there could be greater ramifications. And Sir Walter Scott has made great preparations for the visit. *You canna say no.* The poor man has barely slept."

"Humph…."

The two men continued walking up the hill toward the fairy circle in silence. Out here on the hill they could be themselves, say what they liked. Fairy Hill was a traditional place of magic, but Duncan knew that no magic existed despite the family traditions. It was called Fairy Hill because it had always been called Fairy Hill.

He was an educated man. A man of enlightenment. His father and mother had seen to that. So of course, he did not believe in magic. It may not be a magic hill, but it was the only place on his family lands where he knew in his heart, he was safe from the prying eyes and ears of world around him. This was home. Spending time here always soothed his troubled mind.

He also could look over the land and absorb the most important aspect of the area, its 'Scottishness.' For him it was the land as well as the people and more importantly its real traditions. Traditions that had been denied him since before he was born. Since Culloden and even before that. Traditions that were being threatened as the other lairds cleared the highlands of its people and usual farming practices. By the English who hated them as people. And by a poet who thought that he knew all the traditions of Scotland but took great joy in inventing most of them.

Finally, Duncan broke the silence. "I am going. Does not mean that I must like the idea. And believe me I *dunna*."

He was losing his English drawl. Having been educated at Eton and Oxford as his mother had wanted and having enjoyed the social settings in London, he had returned to Scotland two years ago when his father had died.

He did not mind his mother tongue was returning to the language he loved. He could see that his brother had noticed his slip but had sensibly remained quiet.

They reached the top of the hill and Duncan clenched his fists. Who was the strange lad lying on the fairy rock in the centre of the fairy circle? He let out a quiet curse and went over to the lad and shook his leg. "Wake up laddie and get to where you should be."

Except it was not a lad. It was most definitely a young woman and a beautiful one at that. Her hair was blonde and long but tied behind her head with a ribbon of sorts.

She sat upright staring at him. Her eyes were a piercing blue, reminding him of winter's frozen lake at the big house. He had an immediate reaction to her. Beauty in trousers.

"I understand this is not private land, so I have every right to be here," she said without looking at her accuser. Her legs dangled over the edge of the big rock. If this was a lady, he had never met one like her before. She showed no dignity in the way she sat with her legs wide apart.

"It most definitely is private land." Duncan retorted. "My land, in fact."

Alasdair let out a quiet chuckle.

She rubbed her eyes. "Oh. I'm sorry I must have fallen asleep. The sun has been up for a while, hasn't it?" She stretched and yawned and with her coat open he could see that she had the figure of a woman. The tight shirt she wore held no mystery. Her expression changed from annoyance to confusion. She was looking at him from his head to his boots.

"Are you filming a movie here?" Her eyes darted around. "Great outfits."

"Are you looking for someone, miss? I apologise, but I believed you to be a lad. I have never seen a lady in trousers before."

"Never seen a lady in trousers?" she chuckled and then continued to laugh out loud. But she stopped short. She got off the rock and began to look around her, turning this way and that.

"This isn't right. Where did these trees come from?" She pointed to them, then wandered toward the decline, looking down at the village, "And the village, it's smaller. Where is the shortbread factory? And the distillery? Do you have screens in place to disguise the landscape? Where is my backpack? I left it just there." She pointed to the base of the rock.

"I'm afraid I do not know what you are talking about, miss."

Alasdair went over to her and gently took her arm. "I am sorry, miss…"

"Get your hands off me." Terror filled her voice. She shook her arm free and turned only to run into Duncan's chest as he stepped in front of her. His arms went around her protectively. She looked up into his green eyes and kept staring deeply.

"I know you. You're a famous actor. What was your name again?"

"No miss, not an actor, a laird." He returned the gaze swimming into the pools of blue.

The terror was still there in her eyes as she lost consciousness.

CASTLE BUIN, ABERLOUR

S cotland Tuesday July 30th, 1822

She immediately sat bolt upright, looking quickly around the room. She was alone. Where on earth was she? She could tell she was in a lavish bedroom. But where?

The walls were of whitewashed stone. To her left was a door to somewhere. Next to the door was a chest of drawers beautifully carved and polished but very old. In front of her was a great big stone fireplace. The fire was not lit. Oil paintings and tapestries hung on the walls. She got up and touched the finely woven material of one of the tapestries. Where was she?

She saw the open window, the source of the light, and it explained why she could hear the birds singing. Two chairs upholstered in leather stood in front of it with a small table nestled between them. Green velvet curtains hung from the opening and from the four-poster bed where she had been laying. She still had her clothes on, though her walking shoes and socks were gone. Her jacket was draped on one of the chairs near the window. She slowly let out the breath that she hadn't known she'd been holding.

Cautiously, avoiding making any noise she tiptoed to the window. The floors were polished wood scattered with throw rugs. Through the window she saw a river. Was it the river Spey? She wasn't sure of anything right now. She closed her eyes and the image of the tall black-haired man with the deep green eyes came to her. That man. Why on earth was she thinking about him? She opened her eyes just as the door behind her opened. And the green-eyed man she had conjured in her thoughts stood in the doorway watching her.

"Are you well, Miss...? I do not want you to swoon before me yet again." He spoke with a slight Scottish lilt. She could sense that he was joking with her. But swoon? Who even uses that word? Well, she did but only in the light of her regency stories. She looked at him again.

"I am fine for the moment." She shook her head. "...never mind. Actually, I'm very angry. How dare you take me to wherever it is that I am? This is kidnapping."

"Did you expect me to leave you on the hill, unconscious? Anyone could have taken advantage of you."

"You included, no doubt."

He sighed and came into the room and closed the door. "I am a gentleman Miss...I would not harm you or any other defenceless female."

She turned and looked around the room again. No light switches nor electric clock. There were candles in a candle holder. She looked up. No light fitting. This was one of the best period movie sets. Everything was authentic or as close to authentic as it could be. She could even see the rolled-up bits of paper tapers, which they had used long ago to help them light their fires and candles. This was a great set. She wondered what movie or TV series they were making.

"I could see the confusion on your face earlier my dear, and I can see it returning now." He stepped forward and took her gently by the elbow and guided her to a chair. She stepped back but could not escape him.

"I am confused. I...I...don't know..." Her head was spinning, and nausea creeped into her stomach. She closed her eyes afraid she would again pass out. His hand touched her arms. Though reluctant, she couldn't stop him from touching her.

"Do you remember where we found you this morning?"

"Yes, on Fairy Hill at Aberlour. I'm not stupid, just dizzy." She sat down and stared at him. "Where am I? Why am I here?"

"You are at my estate, not five miles from Aberlour. So, I can take you back to Fairy Hill if needs be. But some answers to my questions first, please?"

"I just want to get back to my B and B."

"What is a B and B?" He stared at her.

"Yeah. Right." She could not believe him. "I said that I was dizzy, not stupid."

"Very well. Let us begin again."

Her stomach was doing summersaults now. She held her breath and pushed down the rising nausea.

"You know Aberlour. I have not heard any, but locals call it Aberlour. Most English call it Charlestown of Aberlour." He paused and looked deeply into her eyes. "Your accent though would indicate that you are not from Scotland. I assume then that you are not from this area?"

"No, I am not." She was reluctant to say anything else until she found out more of the place.

A jigsaw puzzle began to form in front of her eyes and the picture was an old one. One she had used in her research. One that she had fallen in love with as a teenager. An image of a dark-haired man just like the man in front of her. But that picture had been of a regency gentleman.

You've got to be kidding. This is not a fantasy story she suddenly found herself in. This is not fiction, it's fact. What the hell is going on? I need to find out what is right.

She drew in a breath and tried to relax. "I'm from London." She lied. "What the hell is going on here? Tell me."

"That is a very unusual accent for someone from London."

Closing her eyes, she took a deep breath. "I do a fare bit of travelling."

"I see. Do you have a servant or a companion who travels with you? We saw only you on the hill. We may need to find them."

Why would he ask her a strange question like that? Servant?

You must be kidding.

"I travel alone."

He raised his eyebrow as he looked at her, with utter disbelief written across his face.

"That is hard to believe. Even a married woman travels with someone. A companion. Or a servant." He began to pace the room.

"I will travel alone as much as I want. I don't need anyone. What the hell is this place?" She lifted her hands to her now aching head. "Why aren't you answering my questions?"

He stopped pacing and stood in front of her. "Please excuse my doubt madam, miss, but it is most unusual for a single lady to travel alone especially nowadays with the wars not long..." He paused and she waited for another set of questions. His brow furrowed and deepened.

"Your name please, madam? I will not ask again."

No one knew her name here in Scotland and it was easier if she responded to her own name rather than one, she made up. "Rachael Fielding. And I won't ask again either. Who are you?"

"Thank you, Miss Fielding. Definitely not a Scottish name. Very English, in fact." He seemed to stand taller as he placed his hands behind his back. "I am Duncan Murray. Laird of the Clan Murray of Aberlour. You are in my home Castle Buin. And I do not appreciate liars."

He turned and left the room.

IS SHE REAL?

He lent against the door. She was exasperating. And beautiful. One of the most beautiful women he had ever set eyes on. Her hair the colour of harvested hay. Her eyes were bluer than blue; deep pools of sky fixed on her clear pink face. Slender, petite, and elegant. In trousers. She was also a liar. She was not going anywhere.

Duncan came through the door of his library, to see his sister, Glenna, and his brother, Alasdair waiting for him. He poured himself a drink and went to sit in his chair behind his desk.

"It is a little early for that, is it *no* brother?" Glenna placed her hands defiantly on her hips.

"You are my sister, dear, not my mother."

"Sisters can protect you, brother, better than anyone else. Especially when your mother canna be with you. The fairy folk do also."

Duncan looked away.

"So, you don't believe in fairies? Well, how do you explain her?" Glenna paced the floor. Alasdair was flicking through a book showing little or no interest in his sister or the conversation.

"You saw her Dair, she was dressed in very peculiar clothing. How else do you explain her being there? Except that she is fae."

"She could be from France. The fashions are different there. She may have just gotten off a boat." Alasdair did not even glance up.

"The ocean is two days walk away at least. She has no luggage and no servants, no horses or other form of transportation. Now, can you come up with something a little more believable?" She stood there with her arms crossed, waiting.

"And you think that the fae is more believable?" Duncan shook his head.

She continued. "Then tell us Duncan, what you were able to glean from her."

"She says she knows nothing and is from London. And she is very loud." Duncan was not sure he wanted to talk about their 'guest' at the moment.

Alasdair moved over to the desk and sat in the seat next to it. "Not with that accent. She is no Londoner."

"I'm well aware of that." Duncan snapped. "She is lying. I just do not know why. She says she travels a lot but there is no evidence of that from what I can see, other than her strange clothing. She seems very confused at her being found where we found her. And keeps demanding that I return her to the hill. Have the men found any trace of companions or horses in the area?"

"Not as yet." Alasdair said, shaking his head.

"She has appeared on Fairy Hill with no idea how she got there. Do the fae spring to mind, Duncan?" Glenna raised an eyebrow.

"I suggest you write to Sir Walter Scott, Glenna. I believe he will have more use for your stories than I will."

She began to pace back and forth in front of his desk, again.

He continued. "She could have been robbed and was knocked unconscious. Or she is here to cast doubt on this family in the king's mind. He is probably looking for traitors within the Scottish ranks. As all other English kings have done before him. After all we are all Jacobite's. Remember? I do not trust her or the timing of her arrival."

Magic was not part of this situation. This was fact not fiction. Especially with the sudden announcement that the King of England was coming to Edinburgh. A quick and hasty announcement that bewildered him and confused some of the nobility of Scotland. All except Sir Walter Scott, who had been sending all into turmoil as he prepared for the visit, regardless of the cost. He alone had wanted the king to come.

It has been Scott's wish for years, even when the king was the Prince Regent that Scotland should be on his travel arrangements. Scott had written pamphlets and histories around this visit before any indication had been given that the king was coming. So, when the king finally did announce less than a week ago that he was coming, Scott took charge and had all in hand.

Duncan had hurt his sister with his denials. He stood and took his sister, who was only recently turned eighteen, into his arms and hugged her close.

"I know what you want to believe my dear, but this is not the right time or place for such a discussion."

She looked up at him. "And why not? She is Fae, can't you tell?"

"She is just a woman." He hugged her to himself again. "The Fae are fairy tales, folk law. They are not real." He ran his hand through his hair and let out a deep breath, finding this whole Fae idea ridiculous.

She pushed away from him and scowled. "Do not treat me with such condescension. Believe me, she is not of this world." She turned and stormed out of the room, slamming the door as she went.

"That will not help the situation." Alasdair stared at him.

"I do not have time for childish games or stories, Alasdair. This is serious. We must find out more about this woman. She gave her name as Rachael Fielding. We need to find out what she is doing here. With the king's visit to Edinburgh just two weeks away, we need to get the lady to talk to us."

"You might not like what she has to say." Alasdair came to stand with his brother. "I can get that woman to talk, even sing if you'd let me." Alasdair's rakish smile was disconcerting.

Duncan shook his head. "Your methods might interest some women, my dear brother, but trust me when I say this young woman is more than your match. You will not succeed. Besides, I do not want to go down that path." Duncan slapped him gently on the back and Alasdair left the room. Did he want Alasdair to interrogate Miss Fielding? He really did not know what to think or feel.

It was quiet. Way too quiet for her liking and she was scared. Her pulse had been racing since that man had been in the room. What the hell was she going to do? She took some deep breaths and closed her eyes. She had to stay calm and start to think through things logically. As a lawyer she had been trained to do that.

So that training had better start working.

She took deep breaths. There was no way of escape. She was in a tall tower and the door was locked. She shook her head. This sounded like a plot for a medieval novel if it wasn't happening to her. She calmed her breathing again, but she could not make up her mind as to if she were dreaming or on some movie set. Yes, things had changed on the hill.

Perhaps they were props?

The village had changed.

Trick of the light and screens that blocked her vision?

She was locked in a room that showed no signs of 21st century living.

Old castle still being renovated? Fantastic set for a movie.

The more she thought about it the more unsettled she became.

She shook her head. Movie, time travel, going mad. It had to be one of them. She went and sat down. Then stood again. And none of them made her comfortable.

She sat at the table and looked out the window. There were people wandering around but all in period costume. She had not seen lights or cameras or other movie stuff. No trucks or wires. There were even guys out in the fields. No mechanical equipment in sight. But plenty of horses. She closed her eyes again and listened to the sounds floating in through the window.

Think logically. Focus on now.

Birds singing and calling to each other. Bugs whirring and plopping. No cars in the distance. Horses clomping. No sound of aircraft in the skies. No phones. It was genuinely quiet.

The image of a man again floated into her mind. It was the man who had stood before her moments ago. Tall, dark hair. The most handsome of men she had ever seen. But he could be a kidnapper or something worse? It was then that she remembered the painting. A painting she had found in a junk shop when she had been to Scotland with her parents.

Her mother's voice echoed in her mind.

"Why do you want this unfinished painting?"

"It's the eyes, Mum. Look… They look right into your soul."

She watched as her mother stared at the painting for a moment.

"We could get it cleaned and it might look quite nice in the dining room."

"Oh, Mum please, I want it in my room. Those eyes could entice anyone to write. Don't you think?"

"Well, see how much it costs."

Her mother should never had said that. Cause she immediately ran to the owner of the shop.

Poor man took pity on her crazy fifteen-year-old self. She had explained how she wanted to take the painting home and use him to inspire her writing. He ended up giving her the painting, with his blessing.

Again, she slowed her breathing. She had just seen in the flesh, the doppelganger of the man in the painting. What were the chances? That an old painting would look like someone in Scotland today. A painting of a nobleman in Scotland in the 1800's, looking like someone in the 21st century? A cold chill hit the base of her spine and spread up her back. Now she was scared. She shook her head again.

His green eyes could hold any woman captive. She had loved that painting for years. But now? How could someone with the image of a two-hundred-year-old painting have been standing in front of her? His dark hair curling around his beautifully tied cravat. His green eyes boldly staring at her. It was a painting that she wanted to use as one of her heroes, but she never could. Why? Because she had always adored that painting and wanted to keep it for herself. A picture she had been thinking about as she drifted off to sleep laying on a rock on a hill.

And now she was in this laird's castle? This had to be some very detailed dream. No nightmare. How else could she have conjured him up? Her dream man in her favourite portrait?

She heard the key in the lock again and stood up, ready to battle. God, what the hell was she going to do?

But it was not that man who entered, instead a young woman came into the room. She was dressed in a Regency day dress. Dark pink flowers printed on a very pale pink cotton. The young lady had beautiful auburn hair, and green eyes. The same green eyes she had seen on the man Duncan and in her painting.

"I have brought you some food, my dear. Do the fae get hungry? My name is Glenna. Though you are probably aware of that." She placed a tray of food on the small table that was between the chairs near the window. A servant followed and placed another tray with a tea pot and other paraphernalia on it.

Rachael kept her distance.

The poor girl must be nuts. She called me the fae.

For the hundredth time she looked to see if she could see a camera.

Might be some strange reality show.

"Can you tell me your name again?" Rachael made no movement toward her. Her head was beginning to hurt again. This was getting stranger by the minute. And she did not like where her thoughts were going.

"Glenna Murray. My brothers found you upon Fairy Hill. I know many people do not believe in the fae, but I am not one of them. Please sit down and eat." Glenna closed the door and sat in one of the chairs by the window.

Rachael just stared at her. Duncan's sister. The girl believed in fairies.

"Everybody wants to forget there are older mysteries in the world. I am not one of those people. You ken?" Glenna smiled sweetly.

You can do this. Talk to her. Go along with her.

"Can you tell me the reason why you think I am a fae?" Rachael looked at the array on the table and remembered she had not eaten this morning. She planned to have breakfast when she returned from her dawn visit on the hill.

What time was it?

Glenna poured some tea in the cups. "You were found on Fairy Hill. Everyone in the clan know the stories and mysteries surrounding that hill." She handed one of the cups to Rachael.

Rachael came over and took it from her hand.

Okay, let's play this your way.

"Yes, but I do not. I know of no stories or history. I do not know your clan. I know I was near Aberlour and then I woke up here. Where am I now?" She took a sip, then took a large mouthful of the hot sugared liquid.

"Well, I am happy to enlighten you. You are on the lands of the Murray Clan. Our land borders the land owned by the Grants. They have created a bigger village on the site of the small village of Aberlour. Our family still call it Aberlour but Charles Grant who redeveloped it ten years ago calls it Charlestown of Aberlour."

"I didn't know that." She was still very weary and did not take her eyes from the girl sitting in front of her. She drank some more tea.

"Well, if you are not from around here, I imagine you would not."

"Who owns the hill I was found on?"

"We do." Glenna picked up the teapot and poured some more tea into hers and Rachael's cup.

"But I thought the hill was part of the village?"

"No, it is definitely our land. My brother likes the hill and often walks to it and spends time looking down to the Spey and village. It comforts him since our papa died." For the first time since Glenna entered the room, the smile she had on her face disappeared. Rachael watched as Glenna looked out the window and for a moment seemed to be lost in her thoughts before she continued. "My brother, who carried you here, some two miles," she said proudly, "is the laird now. The other man with him on the hill this morning was my other brother Alasdair."

Rachael was silent for a moment as they both sipped their tea.

"And do you have any other family here in your home? Or should I say castle?" She took another deep breath and held it, to slow her breathing. The fear racking her since she had awakened was still not under her control.

Glenna laughed. "Yes, this is an old castle. You are in the tower that used to be part of the original keep. It dates to the 12th century. My father has done extensive renovations to it, however. He very much valued our history as my brother continues to do. And I have another brother but he's away from home."

This was all very interesting information, but she needed to come to a solution to her immediate problem.

Was this a movie set?

"Can I ask you to tell me what kind of film you are making here?"

"I do not know what you mean. What is a film?"

Oh, the girl was really nuts.

She ignored the question and tried another tack.

"Can you tell me the history of the hill? And what it is that makes you think I am of the fae?" Rachael lifted the teacup to her lips and took a sip. It was hot and strong but had done nothing to sooth her troubled thoughts.

"Very well. Let me think. For centuries, my family have lived on this land. The hill has always been known as the Fairy Hill. Stories of family members disappearing and never being seen again have abounded. Also, strangers who would appear. And always from the direction of the hill."

"Strangers. Strangers like me?"

"This is the first time it has happened since I was born. The stories say that they were always dressed differently and spoke with unusual accents. Some spoke English and others, languages that my family could not understand."

"If you believe the stories have happened, that they are true, then how…does it happen?"

"Well, the stories say that the stones on top of the hill make up a fairy ring. If you look carefully when you stand on the hill you can see that they form a circle or ring shape. Some of the stones are small and go unnoticed. Then there is the big stone in the middle of the circle. About three foot high. Then I imagine it's the usual things that can happen in a fairy ring."

Rachael took a deep breath and slowly let it out. "What can happen in the fairy ring? I don't know any fairy stories from around here." She studied the young girl's face to see if she could ascertain any dishonesty. She could not see anything else than truth. The girl believed her stories.

"Let me think…You should never be in the ring after sunset or at dawn, nor fall asleep in the ring at any time. The fairies can come and take who they like should anyone disobey these instructions. After all it is their ring. They can then take you back to their land or wherever they deem you should be."

"Should be?" Rachael was finding it hard to stay still. She got up for a moment and walked to the other side of the room and then came back to sit down. She picked up her cup and drank some more tea. The warm brew might calm her yet and give her some solace.

Glenna continued. "Yes. If you made a wish or had thought that you should be somewhere else, while on the hill, then that is enough for them to act. Change your life. But only if you're in the ring when they come looking."

Rachael put down the cup. She had gotten into the ring before sun rise and had sat on the three-foot rock in its centre. Took photos, contemplated, and dreamed. She had wanted things to change. A new life. She had wished Josh dead to her. Then she had fallen asleep as the sun slowly rose, after her call from Sam. On the rock. Dreaming of a Scotsman to come into her life. A tall dark and handsome Scotsman. The man in her painting.

"Are you alright, Rachael? You have gone very pale."

Rachael hesitated, staring at Glenna. "I would like to go to the bathroom please."

"What is a bathroom? If you wish to bathe, I can get the servants to bring up the bath. I am not sure what you mean by bathroom?"

"I want to relieve myself, go to the toilet. You know."

Glenna stood and went to the bed and reached underneath it. "I think you wish to use this. I can leave the room while you relieve yourself. I will call for a servant to come and take it away."

"This isn't funny anymore."

Glenna smiled as she left the room.

Rachael was busting and really needed to go. So, she did. Why would they do this to her? Things were getting out of hand. After a moment she opened the door and Glenna came straight in followed by a maid who picked up the pot and left the room. Another servant entered with a jug and large bowl.

"I thought you might like to freshen up. I will leave you to it. Rachael? Are you well?"

Rachael stood there. The way Duncan and his brother had been dressed? The way Glenna was dressed like she had come straight out of the pages of a Jane Austen novel? There was no mistaking it. She was in another time. It wasn't a movie set. She was not mad. She had been sent back in time by the fairies…

WHOSE REALITY?

The door opened and Duncan came in. "What are you doing in here?" he asked his sister.

"I was meeting Rachael and finding out about her. And welcoming the fae among us."

Rachael's head began to spin. "I do not feel at all well. I need to lay down."

"Of course." A note of concern entered his voice. "Is there anything I can get you?" He helped her over to the bed.

She let him. His touch upset her more, but she lay down, pushing back again the sensation she was about to throw up.

Duncan quietly addressed his sister. "Meet me down in the library, go now please." Glenna carried the tea tray out of the room without saying a word. Another servant entered and cleared away the remaining items.

Rachael pulled her legs up to her chest. He placed a quilt over her body that she drew closer to herself.

"I will return in a few hours so we can talk again. Try to sleep. I hope you will be feeling better."

She heard his footsteps on the wooden floor and heard the

clicks as the door shut and was locked. She again found herself alone and a prisoner. A prisoner, in a castle in another time? She pulled the quilt over her head and wept.

Standing on the opposite side of the door he heard her sob. He needed to talk with his sister and find out what they had spoken about. She was so pale when he entered the room, he thought she had died. He walked to the head of the stairs, but Rachael's weeping could still be heard.

"I am not angry. I just might have found it useful if I had been in the room with you." Duncan was pacing the carpet in front of the fireplace in his library.

"But you were so angry and suspicious of her that I thought she needed to hear a friendly word. She would never have been so open if you had been there. You saw how quiet she was when you came in."

Glenna stood very still.

He needed to make things right. He wanted this woman who had appeared out of nowhere to tell him more than she had. But in her current condition that would not happen.

He sighed deeply. "I suggest that we ask Miss Fielding to have dinner with us tonight. I want to make her feel she is a guest. Not an enemy or a prisoner."

"I think that is a wonderful idea, Duncan. But I am not sure she will want to. She is also very suspicious. And now she seems to be quite ill."

"I do not trust her, Glenna. So, it would seem we are both suspicious of each other. But at the moment she seems vulnerable and I do not want to distress her anymore."

I would rather gain her confidence. Find out why she was really here.

"I'm sorry Glenna. It would appear you have been more civil than I have. Your behaviour was impeccable. Thank you for your help."

His sister stood looking as if he had stepped into a new time and place. He very rarely apologised for anything but had to concede that he needed to now if the information he wanted was to be obtained.

"I will go through my older dresses and see what I can find that she might fit into. She is not as tall as I am now, but I should be able to find something for her. If...that is suitable with you, brother." She waited patiently.

"Of course. Do what you feel is right. You might ask Mrs Gibb to see which of the servants might be assigned to her. We must amend our behaviour and make her welcome."

"Thank you, Duncan. I am sure she will repay us for your kindness. She really is a poor lost soul." She hugged her brother.

Quietly, because all his anger was spent, he added, "I don't think she is a fae despite what you believe. There will be a logical and sensible explanation for why she was found where she was."

"Yes, Duncan. Whatever you say." She gave him another hug and left the room.

Tales from the past had a lot to answer for when it came to his sister. He could not understand why his father had encouraged the stories to be told.

He sat behind his desk and pondered Miss Fielding. The beautiful, blue eyed vision of perfection that had dropped into his lap. From somewhere.

Who was she? What was she?

MAGIC?

The golden light coming through the window told Rachael they were nearing the end of the day. She had to get out of this room and get to the circle now the sun was going down. Her head still hurt.

The knock at the door drew her out of her thoughts. Duncan Murray and his sister came into the room. She closed her eyes and waited for the attack to begin.

"Miss Fielding, I hope you are feeling better?" Glenna came over to the bed and touched her forehead.

Rachael had to gain their confidence if she was going to get out of this room and back to the ring. *Be nice.*

"Thank you, I am. I am sorry for my...turn." She sat up on the bed.

"That is not a problem at all. You were obviously most unwell. I am glad to see you are feeling better. The colour has returned to your cheeks."

This man was all sweetness! What the...?

"If I can be so presumptuous," Glenna intruded on Rachael's

thoughts. "I have arranged for a bath and a change of clothing. They may contribute to your wellbeing."

"Then if you would join us for dinner...?" Duncan looked longingly at her and she felt a kick in her midriff. Surely, she was not attracted to this man. He had been rude and aggressive, and he had kidnapped her. Her stomach was churning not for attraction but hatred she concluded.

"That would be very nice." Why was she being polite to him? She turned to look at Glenna. "Thank you for your kindness." And she meant it. Glenna had only been kind, even if fairies were the reason for the kindness.

Duncan bowed. "Then I will take my leave so you can prepare for dinner. I would like to hear all about where you came from." He smiled, a smile full of suspicion and left the room.

As Duncan left, two footmen walked in carrying an old-fashioned bath made of highly polished copper. A maid had followed them in, laid down an old blanket on the floor. The footmen placed the bath on top of it and left the room. Then maids came in quick succession carrying small buckets of hot water they emptied into the bath. Another maid lit the fire in the fireplace.

"I will leave a maid in the corridor so you can call if you want more water added or are ready to rinse off. Then after your bath, your maid Morag will help you dress, as well as do your hair. I hope that is suitable?"

"More than suitable. Though I can dress myself. And what do you mean—my maid?"

"While you are here Duncan wishes you to have use of a maid. And I have found you a dress that I hope will fit you." She turned to leave, "Oh and remember, Morag will be waiting outside."

Glenna left. Rachael waited until the bath was filled and the door closed to undress slowly and enter the bath. No bathroom in the house? The water was divine, and she sank into it. The bath was surprisingly bigger than it looked, and she wallowed in the warmth the water sent through her body. On a little table that had been carried in, was a cloth and a bar of soap. She picked it up and brought it to her nose and took a deep breath. Lavender.

Rachael washed herself and tried to remember the things they had discussed about the fairies. She had to get away but with time to get away unseen. She had to admit that the evidence so far led her to believe that she had travelled back in time. Crazy but true. Accepting that gave her a sense of relief.

"Well I must say that the dress looks better on you than it ever did on me." Glenna had entered the room. Rachael was standing at the window watching the light of the moon spread over the highlands.

Dreamlike and magical. It was like she was dreaming despite the physical realities of the bath, the touch of the clothing and the maid's preparations of her hair. Seeing the refection of her face in the window thanks to the candles lit by the maid, she was looking wonderful. This period of time she had adored. Writing about regency was enthralling for her and now here she was standing in the history for herself and not wanting to go anywhere. Certainly not home to her own time. This really was nuts.

Why was she thinking like this?

Rachael was glad Glenna couldn't read minds. She had come to the window to see how she could attempt her escape. But looking over the beautiful scene she had started thinking…

Perhaps she could stay for a while?

No one would miss her. Her parents were gone. Her friends in Dubbo knew that she was staying away for at least three months. She was on a retreat from the world. She gave a short chuckle. She could enjoy, even for a short time, this world that she had always adored. Sam would know that she was out of things for a while. She wouldn't get worried straight away. What a great way to do research. Living it. Meanwhile she could win their confidence and eventually find the right time to get back to the ring on the hill and go home. Perhaps...

Glenna was standing behind her fixing a curl that needed adjusting in her 'coiffeur'.

She hid a smile. She was even thinking the language. She could stay for a while. Couldn't she? This morning she was in fear but now she had accepted that she was out of her own time. These people didn't know that. They might just see her as a lost soul. She looked at Glenna and smiled.

"Thank you for the dress. It is beautiful."

"Red was never a colour I liked. And it made me look too old. But on you," she quickly corrected "it looks wonderful."

"I will take that as a compliment. I think." She looked at Glenna who looked stunning in the gold silk dress that embraced her tall slender form. She smiled again and received a glorious grin in return.

"Please do. I do not give them to just anyone, believe me." Then she laughed with such joy that Rachael knew she not only liked the young lady who stood behind her but believed they would be friends. This morning she had feared her but now she wanted to trust her.

Glenna had already been so generous. She had tried on many dresses and two of Glenna's maids had left a while ago with their arms full of dresses and other items that just needed mild alterations to allow her to wear them. She spent a great deal of time thinking about Duncan in the last few hours and wanted to know more. Why was he so angry? And it was easier to be herself around Glenna than the man from the painting.

"May I ask you some questions before we go down?"

"I will answer to the best of my ability." She smiled at her and Rachael smiled back. There seemed to be a connection between them.

"It is your brother, Duncan. To put it bluntly he is an angry young man. Why is he so angry? Not just at me but generally. It seems to be part of his nature. I am sorry to be so blunt."

Glenna looked at her, took her by the hand and drew her to the chairs to sit down. "You can see all his anger? And that it is not directed to just you? And you say you are not fae?" She paused for a moment. "You are correct. My brother has taken the duties of the laird very seriously. He feels the pain of our people. But he has taken on more pain than he should. He is concerned for the whole of Scotland. And that is a lot of pain to bear."

Rachael nodded.

"He has watched my father's anguish over our clan, as numerous clans around us break up and leave the shores of Scotland." She paused and was deep in thought for a moment. She continued. "Duncan has been well educated. Our mother saw to that. But unlike many others he came home while others have gone with their clans over the seas. I think, from what he has said and knows, Scotland could have been a different place, if we had our independence from the English. But as you know we lost at Culloden and we lost so much more than just our independence. He does not trust the English nor the king and that is a seed deeply rooted in the family. Many Scots feel that way. He is not the only one." She looked out through the window and into the darkened sky. "When you're in deep pain you end up trusting no one."

"Thank you, Glenna. That helps me to understand his anger. Perhaps he will see, in time that I pose no threat to him or your clan. He found me in the wrong place and the wrong time."

Glenna smiled knowingly at her.

Rachael could see Glenna's profound insights. For someone so young, she was very wise. She also knew her brother well. Aha, now she could understand Duncan better. There was no doubt about it. This was the past and she had to learn to live in it. At least for now.

Would she ever hear what has happened to the clan over the years, from Duncan himself, now that she planned to stay a while? Yes, she would stay a while. She had decided. She wanted to know more. She wanted Duncan to tell her of his feelings and anger. The man in the portrait had beaconed her and she had come. Or had her desire been the only reason? She still feared him, but her interest had been pricked.

Glenna took her hand and laced into her own. "Come, let us go to dinner and stun the gentleman folk."

The walk down the stairs helped to draw Rachael into the world she loved. The stairwell was ancient. It was freshly whitewashed but made of stone. She could see the ancient bones of the building and was fascinated. This was no movie set unless they were in a real castle. She laughed at herself as she still doubted her decision of believing she was in the past. Her observations continued. The old rope attached to the wall acted as a banister was real. She touched it reverently. How many other hands over the centuries had touched it?

"That floor has other guest rooms." Glenna pointed to the flight of stairs from which they descended. "And the ground floor has the library." She pointed toward the library as they came to the bottom step. Rachael looked from side to side and could see that the old tower was square at its base. "These doors lead to the new part of the castle." Glenna continued, then pointing to the right. "The others to the outside."

Rachael noted the manservants at both doors. No escape from either way. To the left stood some great oak doors. The light golden honey colour stood out against the whitewashed walls. These doors were to the main part of the house. The footman opened them wide and stood to the side as they went through. Rachael stopped and looked about her. The décor was that of a great house of England. It was very Georgian, and she guessed it was built to feel like a great English house. The door of the tower closed quietly behind them.

"This is strange." Rachael added. "This feels very English not Scottish."

"Ah, that was my mother's doing. She comes from Scottish ancestry, a Buchanan, but lived all her life in London. At least till she married father. Father is a Murray as you know and a very wealthy one. He had made much money as a merchant as well as on Murray lands. So, he added this part to the old castle just for her. So that she could feel at home."

Rachael slowly walked down the hall toward the dining room. She stopped along the way to look at paintings hanging on the wall, vases set on pedestals and the carpet clinging to the polished wooden floors. Everything was right, true, and so accurate for a regency house. The tower was so Scottish, but this part of the castle could have been found in any London townhouse of the regency period.

Rachael could tell Glenna was watching her carefully, as she showed her interest in the things along the way. If they had a story attached to them, she stopped to tell Rachael about it. It was for friendship that she answered all her queries. There was no malice or suspicion, unlike her experiences with Duncan. There was great curiosity. That was it. No more no less.

The door opened at the end of the hall and the two ladies drifted quietly into the dining room. The candlelight spread a glow of golden radiance across the room and the huge reddish-brown mahogany dining table. Two gentlemen stood as they came in and Rachael recognised Duncan and guessed the other gentleman was his brother Alasdair.

Duncan was dressed in the usual dark evening wear of a gentleman. The material had a shimmer to it. His rich jet-black hair was neatly combed back, and his glorious green eyes were fixed on her. She looked back into his gaze and smiled. He returned the smile.

That boded well.

Her gaze drifted to Alasdair. He also was dressed in the evening wear of a gentleman, but his hair was tussled and reckless and very auburn. So different from Duncan. She got the distinct impression that recklessness was a permanent part of Alasdair's persona. His eyes were blue and not as captivating as Duncan's. The way he stood, more relaxed than the formal posture of his brother added to his recklessness. That observation intrigued her but did not distract her from Duncan.

Alasdair came toward them.

"Dair, can I properly introduce you to Miss Fielding?" Glenna was smiling and relaxed.

"Charmed, I'm sure. We met very briefly on the hill. But we were not properly introduced."

Rachael gave a small curtsey and was immediately convinced that Alasdair did all the charming in this house. He took her hand and lifted it to his mouth. He laid a gentle kiss on her fingertips.

"It is a pleasure to meet you properly, my dear."

She was sure that her face revealed her a traitor. She had been moved by his compliments. He was handsome and charming and reminded her of Josh. She frowned just a little. Josh had a way of charming everyone, especially the females. She was not going to be taken in by the handsome man who stood before her. She had learned her lessons from Josh. She removed her hand from his and turned to face Glenna.

Duncan pulled out the chair next to him and his sister came over and sat down. Alasdair returned to the table and pulled out the chair next to him and Rachael drifted over to it and sat down. She had no choice. She had to sit next to Alasdair. She would need to be sure not to be taken in by his attentions. But this seat placed her directly opposite Duncan.

That is wonderful, not!

She could spend the evening being cross examined by a man who didn't trust her and be flirted with by a well-practiced rake. The compensation was she could stare into the forest green eyes of the man who distrusted her. Eyes that she had already wanted to stare at her for the rest of her life. And not just from a painting. Not a great place to be.

Wrong place, wrong time, literally.

LIVING THE DREAM

The food was exquisite. Each course was an image of perfection. The aromas bombarding the room were mesmerising. It was like she was in a high-class restaurant. And despite her fears of being interrogated, the conversation was pleasant and cordial. They discussed the weather, the state of the roads and how Hamish, brother number three, was doing in Edinburgh. She said little but listened intently so she could understand and take note of the world into which she had been dropped. If she had her doubts before, they were gone now. She was in the past. No more second guessing.

After dinner they wandered down the hall and back into the tower to sit in the library. The room was a traditional library full of books from all around the then known world. She wandered from shelf to shelf examining the great works on display. But it soon became obvious that Duncan wanted her to talk. Not just about the weather. He wanted to know more about her. Why she was there? His attitude and mood swiftly changed from the pleasant host to the soldier's posture she had seen before.

"Miss Fielding, will you now be able to tell us how you came to be on our land?"

Rachael took a deep breath and tried to keep calm. She wanted to be as truthful as possible without revealing what she had come to believe as the truth. Time travel was not something these people would understand let alone accept.

Heck, she could hardly believe it. Did they still burn witches?

She came over to the table and accepted a cup of tea Glenna had poured for her and sat on the lounge chair next to her.

"To tell you the truth Mr Murray, I honestly am not sure how I got here. On the hill, I mean." She was, in part, telling the truth. After all who else would accept that fairies were involved in time travel.

"Please understand me, Miss Fielding. I saw the anguish and shock on your face this afternoon and I know that something is not right. I do not know what upset your sensibilities. I only want to protect my family and estate. Do you understand? So, please tell me why you are here."

Rachael placed the teacup she had in her hand on the table in front of her. "Sir, I swear I do not know why I am here. I can't be sure how I got here. Other than you bringing me to your castle I don't know much of where I am. I do not know why you would fear me even if I could recall. All I remember is falling asleep and waking where you found me." She lifted her gaze to look at him directly, into his green eyes. Oh, she so wanted him to believe in her.

Duncan stood from the chair he was sitting in and came to stand before her. He never for a moment took his eyes off her. "I have tried to be patient. I have tried to welcome you with kindness and all you do is lie to me. This will not do."

"I'm sorry, Mr Murray. I am not lying. I have nothing else to say. I am confused and unsure of what has happened to me. I know who I am but that is all. This is not what I expected. I am out of my comfort zone." She dropped her gaze. She did not want to investigate his face. His angry untrusting face. *Why would he not believe her?*

"Miss Fielding, my brother and I are merely trying to determine how you came to be on our Fairy Hill." Alasdair's tone was gentle, but he was staring at her with utter confusion on his face. It seemed he wanted the truth just as much as his brother. But he was calmer than Duncan.

What was she going to do?

She got up and went to stand before the bookcase. Duncan followed, coming to stand before her. Alasdair too, stood and came to stand next to Duncan. Were they trying to intimidate her? Yes? Well, it was working. She wanted to run from the room screaming. Instead she stared at the highly polished boots standing in front of her.

"If you could all calm yourselves, I will gladly give you my opinion." Glenna came over, took her hand, and squeezed it. Rachael could see everyone around her, and she was surrounded. She placed her other hand to her head and was suddenly dizzy. But Duncan was oblivious to his attitude and his growing temper. He reeked of malice and danger. Why on earth was he so angry? She had done nothing except appear.

"Sister. Enough of these foolish stories. You are making an absolute fool of yourself. Please stay out of this discussion." Duncan had raised his voice. Rachael lifted her head to see that his face was red and it seemed to her, as if he were ready to explode. Now the delights of the evening had been shattered. There was only hatred in his eyes and that rocked her to her core.

"The truth is sir...is that you wouldn't know the truth if it stood in front of you, to bite you. Glenna is right. I came here thanks to the hospitality of the fairies. I'm from the future. So, how do you like the truth now?" She placed her hands firmly on her hips. Glenna stood next to her, mimicking her stance.

"Do not involve my sister in your treachery."

"What treachery? I have no idea what you mean. What is it that you think I am? Do you think me a spy or a witch?" She took a deep breath. Who cares if they plan to burn her at the stake? She would be home before that. "Really, I am tired of this. I have no idea why you think being on the Fairy Hill suddenly makes me treacherous. I have had it up to here. I want to go home. Yes, my home in the future. I know you don't believe me, but I don't care."

Her anger was real and so was her courage. She went in boots and all and wanted to get as much info out of him as she could. When she finally sat down to write her next story, it was going to be unbelievable.

"What year is it anyway? Can someone please tell me that? I haven't been game to ask before now."

They all stared at her with utter confusion plastered on their faces. No, not quite. Alasdair was staring at her is if she were mad. She could almost smell the smoke of the flames she imagined lapping around her. She was going to burn as a witch.

"1822." Glenna answered before either of her brothers became distracted. Glenna crossed her arms and stood there with the biggest smirk on her face.

"But you know that. Don't you?" Duncan yelled. "Stop pretending that you are unaware of the year. This is utter foolishness. Travelling in time is nonsense." Duncan ran his fingers through his hair. She waited for him to pull his hair out in big clumps.

She went and sat back into her chair. Glenna followed. "If that is the case, then I need to think." So, she started thinking out loud while keeping her eyes closed. "The Napoleonic wars are finished. King George 4th would be on the throne now, his regency finished. Jane Austen is dead. Blast. Won't be meeting her. Scotland, Scotland...let me think..." Rachael's thoughts ran through all the different books she had read as part of her research.

"What nonsense is this? Those things are common knowledge.

What use, if any, is the year to you? Why would you ask such a ridiculous question?" She could see that Duncan was getting angrier by the minute. And she was sure he was ready to explode. She took in a deep breath and looked him directly, into the green eyes.

"I am trying to remember any details of this period that might be useful. Hopefully then you might believe me. The only thing I can remember in relation to Scotland is the Kings Jaunt. A book by Prebble about the king's visit to Edinburgh."

"What do you know of the king's visit?"

Well, well. That hit a nerve.

Duncan continued. "So, you are aware of his coming. It has all been organised at very short notice. They have been saying he has been coming for years but have only recently announced the dates. Tell me what you know?" Duncan had grabbed her by her upper arms. Glenna grabbed hold of her hand.

It was obvious to her; she had remembered the wrong thing. His hatred for the English King was now clear to her. She desperately tried to remember anything that might help her. She closed her eyes again.

"Duncan please, this is ridiculous. Surely you can see that she knows more because she comes from another time and place." Glenna held Rachael's hand, gently squeezing it to reassure Rachael that she was not alone. Rachael opened her eyes and went on trying to get Duncan to see reason.

Reason, what the hell was that?

"Let me think. I can't remember. The king came, Scott, the poet and author was involved in all the organising and he turned the history of Scotland on its head. Far too romantic for his own good, that man. Oh, he got all dressed up in what he called traditional kilt wear. The king too. Yes, and the trip was organised in two weeks." Rachael watched as his face grew redder as the seconds passed.

"You're here because the king is looking to make us more

submissive than we already are. It is a plot to disgrace us yet again. Isn't it?" He was shaking her. Not too much but enough to concern her.

"You really don't know that the king is enamoured by the stories of Scott and wants to enjoy all that Scotland can supply, do you? He will end up loving Scotland. And so, will his niece Victoria."

"And how do you know what the king is thinking unless he sent you to spy on us? What do you have to do with the royal family? And who in God's name is Victoria?" His grip tightened.

"What on earth…its history, leave me alone." She tried to get away from his grip.

"Yes, it is clear now. You are spying for the king because he plans to come here and humiliate the Scots further. He wants to subjugate Scotland even more." Duncan was yelling and his face was red with rage.

"Brother, I think that you have gone too far. Listen to the way she is speaking, as if it has already happened." Glenna wanted him to see.

She needed to convince them, but she feared the look in Duncan's eyes. "You truly are crazy, mad. I don't know the king. Just the history. Let me leave here and return to my own time. I promise you; you will never see me again. I won't come back. Promise."

Duncan froze, still gripping her by the tops of her arms. His eyes closed and she could imagine his thoughts turning inward.

He moved her toward his brother. "Take her upstairs and lock her in the room. We need to work out what we are going to do with her. This witch."

"Don't lock me up again. You can't keep me prisoner. It's illegal. You're taking away my liberty. It's against the Geneva Convention. Please, I am not a witch…" But it was too late. Alasdair had her by the arms and had moved her to the doorway as if she was a rag doll. Glenna was weeping as she followed her.

"Sister, come away from her." Duncan demanded.

"No. You cannot treat her in such an infamous manner. She is no witch. Please let her go."

Duncan only had to say one word. "Glenna…"

Glenna dropped Rachael's hand immediately. But her tears and cries did not stop. Rachael heard her return to the lounge and sob, begging him to stop.

Alasdair took her from the room and escorted her up the stairs and not so gently. She could hear the sobs of Glenna and cursed herself for opening her stupid mouth. Now she was to die like all the other Scottish witches. But it was 1822. They didn't burn witches.

No, they probably sent them all to Australia as convicts.

Quietly she pleaded, "Please Alasdair, don't lock me up."

"I must but only till I can calm him. Trust me, please."

They continued walking up the stairs.

"Why should I trust you? You think I am a witch."

"That is the last thing that you could be. I do not believe in fairies or witches. I need to calm him. It is better that I try to do that with you out of the room. Again, I ask you to trust me. I will protect you."

"I bet. You're another Josh."

He looked at her with a distinct frown on his face. "I do not know what you mean but I will protect you." She lowered her head and continued the aching walk up to her prison.

She heard the key again turn as she fell on her bed. She was in a mess and could not see a way out. She wanted to cry but she was all cried out. How could she now escape? Certain that she would now die, or worse, she lay there trembling at the darkness of her room.

After her eyes had adjusted to the gloom she got up and went to the window. Staring out into the moon-lit night, she wished every fairy that was on the planet would carry her home.

You started this, guys. You had better fix it. I might be a lawyer, but I can't talk my way out of this one.

DO I BELIEVE HER?

"Duncan, here drink this."

Alasdair handed him a glass of whisky. It had more than his usual. Was his brother trying to make him drunk?

"I'm not saying she isn't a spy but let us look at the facts, please?"

"What facts are there brother, that she is fae?" He paced back and forth in front of his desk. He looked at his sister who sat quietly on the same lounge that Rachael had recently been seated. Her head was bowed, and she quietly sniffed.

Alasdair went on ignoring his sarcasm. "She is definitely not from London," he held up one finger on his left hand.

"We can all see and hear that…"

But Alasdair would not let him continue. "For once take council from me, brother."

Turning his head, he stared at his brother. Alasdair had very strong opinions but very rarely voiced them. He always did what was asked of him even if he may not have agreed with him. Now he stood before him with his feet slightly apart and one hand behind his back. He could see that he had no intention of budging. He seemed ready for a fight. If Alistair had not been holding up his other hand showing one finger, he would have easily imagined his fist heading for his face. He just could not understand why he was defending Rachael.

Duncan moved to the other side of his desk and sat down. He slammed his hands on the desk. But he stopped himself from getting angrier because he didn't want to display it in front of his family. And he had no reason to explain why, other than Rachael. Her image appeared before his mind's eye and he closed his eyes to absorb her beauty. She had bewitched him. There was no other explanation. Perhaps she was a fae? Or at least a witch.

"I repeat," he held his hand in front of him. "She is not from London. Two, she had very unusual shoes and clothing when we found her."

Duncan's eyes opened and he bored his gaze into Alasdair. Why was his brother stating the things they already knew? Alasdair would not give ground.

"Three, she has a great deal of knowledge, current yes, but more than is usual for a woman."

"I beg your pardon?" It was time for his sister to object and he had to agree. As their sister, she had never been afraid to voice her opinions.

"Let me finish, please. She is educated if you prefer. And some information that she revealed is very obscure. Is there a Princess Victoria? I do not pay much attention to the royal family and its lineage. We might need to find out more about that. And what the hell is the Geneva Convention? Four, she has knowledge of the king's visit so she must be in the circle of Scott or the king or a clan close to the king. Very few others know or even care. The news has only just reached us. Five, she has no idea how she got to the hill and she was telling the truth on that score. You saw her confusion on the hill as well as I did. But there is more." He lifted his hand to stop all from saying any more. "What of the bewildered look that she revealed on her face when Glenna told her the year. Then the relief as if she had already accepted that she had come a longer way than she had first thought. No one could act that well. It was real. She believes she is from the future. I don't know why but she does." Alasdair looked at his hand with all five fingers showing.

"How can you believe her?" Duncan stared at his brother, pleading for an answer. "I see no truth, but you say that you do. Yet this morning you were convinced she was a spy."

"I have not made up my mind as to her state of mind but you, brother, have. You have sentenced her before you have even asked if the truth she tells, is the truth or lies. You brother, have already condemned her."

Duncan almost stopped breathing. It was if Alasdair had hit him in his midriff. Alasdair spoke the truth. He had condemned her. He had made her part of a plot, any plot. Her truth could never be his truth.

That was why he did not want to be laird because he could not read people, know them, the way his brother could. Pick their moods, detect the truth or the lies. The way his father had. He took a deep breath and lowered his gaze. He was ashamed. This is not the way his father would behave. The room remained quiet as his sister and brother waited for his response.

"If we accept what you say, what do we do now?" Duncan lifted his head. He could see his sister could not take her eyes off him. He had never conceded to his brother before but here he was doing just that. And they were waiting to hear his reply. Alasdair did not disappoint.

"That, my dear brother, and sister, is simple. She is a woman and we need to show her that we believe her. We pretend to believe her story that she is from the future. At least for now."

"But I do believe her." Glenna exalted. "You either do or you don't."

"I see." And Duncan could. It suddenly seemed extremely clear.

By believing her they could or would eventually find out the truth. Alasdair was nodding knowingly at his brother. "Very well. I am prepared to see your side of this."

"Duncan, she is telling the truth." The look on his sister's face showed very clearly that she believed who she thought Rachael was. He would let her. She had already befriended the woman. She could get closer to her than the rest of them. She could get the information that he sought.

"She may be telling the truth or at least what she believes is truth. I am prepared to believe her. But it would help us greatly if we could get more information from her, to help me to believe it. Some evidence if you like?" He hoped his sister would believe he wanted the change even if he really did not. "It is a story even she is finding difficult to believe. She trusts you and would probably tell you more than she would tell us."

"I will not lie to her and I will not spy for you. I will tell you anything that makes me believe that she is from the future. From the fae if you prefer. That is all. Do not ask me to do otherwise. I believe in her and the fae." With that Glenna stood, curtseyed, and left the room.

At least she was calmer and did not leave in a huff as she had before. He also had no doubt that she would tell Rachael that they were pretending to believe in her. That meant that he and Alasdair had to be convincing, to get her to believe in them. Getting any information out of her was going to be difficult.

"What do you suggest that we do from this point?" Duncan was prepared to listen to Alasdair's point of view. He still wished that his brother could be laird and that he could return to the studies he had left behind at Oxford.

"We let her out of the room. Give her the freedom of the house and the gardens. But one of us will always be by her side. She will never be left to her own devises." Alasdair stood there with ease. He was convinced if nothing else that his plan would work.

He was prepared to give his brother's plan a chance but doubted this woman would fall into their little trap. He was cautious and needed to see everything was in place and would work. "But that will place enormous pressure on us. We still have an estate to run and the king's visit! We need to leave for Edinburgh in a week."

"That is simple." Alasdair continued. "At night, her room can be watched by a servant and we can be awakened if she should try to escape." Alasdair paused and smiled a devilish grin at his brother. "I will slip in her bed if you would like? I'm sure that I can keep her well occupied and make her talk." Alasdair waited patiently for his response.

"If this suggestion of yours is merely to get her into your bed then I tell you now that I will not allow it." Duncan could not stand the thought of his brother placing one hand on her body. Her beautiful, slim, petite body. Her neck, slender and delicate. Her beautiful golden hair—soft and fairylike. He shook his head. "No. No dalliance. Do you understand me?"

"Certainly, Duncan." Alasdair had lost his rakish grin.

He did not trust his brother.

What was he after?

Duncan was not convinced his brother heeded his word or meant what he said. So, he would have to watch him as well. This would make the coming week most difficult. He was concerned that he now could not even trust Alasdair. This woman was driving him to distraction.

"As for Edinburgh," Alasdair continued, "we take her with us. Glenna would be pleased of the company. That way we can determine if she is a plotter, by who pays attention to her or seeks her out. And who she might look for."

Duncan, though cautious, could now see the value in his brother's plan. Duncan went to the bell pull and summoned a footman. He turned back to his brother.

"Very well. Glenna is unaware we will be watching her so

closely. I will arrange for an early meeting with a select group of servants but will arrange a footman to stay outside her door tonight. We can set things in motion properly in the morning. One way or another we will find out about the real Rachael Fielding."

Rachael heard the knock at the door. It had not been long since she had been locked in her room. She heard the lock click. The door opened and Glenna stepped in. The light from the candle that she held reached into the room.

"You shouldn't be sitting here in the dark." Glenna walked to the fireplace and lit the candle on the mantle.

"We have talked some sense into Duncan, but we need to be careful. I believe they plan to watch you, to see what you will do. Be on your guard."

"What do you mean watch me? What did they say?"

"They will tell you they believe your story, to win your confidence. I do not know what else they have planned. It is my guess that they will watch you. Regardless of what they are planning, know that I am your friend and will protect you."

Rachael stared at her new friend. She was bewildered as to why Glenna wasted her time on her. "Why would you do that? They are your family. I am a stranger to you. Your brothers will not be happy."

Glenna smiled and sighed. She came over to her and hugged her. "Trust me please. I will talk with you more tomorrow. I need to think more on their possible plans. I think they will allow you out. I will see you at breakfast."

"This makes little sense to me. They don't trust me."

"But I do."

And just as quickly as she had come, she was gone, and the door locked again. Anyone would think that Glenna was the fae the way she moved silently here and there.

Boy, she was going nuts.

Not everyone around her had fairy blood. Well, Duncan certainly didn't fall into that category. What was she to make of it all? Why would Glenna put her relationship with her family at risk to help her? It was confusing. But then the last twenty-four hours had been perplexing.

Rachael changed out of her clothing by candlelight. Then brought the candle to the table next to her bed. She lay there as the candlelight flickered against the wall of her prison. Tomorrow was another day and perhaps she could learn more and then finally make plans to go home. Wanting to stay and observe this world had been a foolish idea. She would never fit in. She couldn't even control her temper. Reaching over to the small table, she blew out the candle. Now, all she could see as the dark gathered around her were a pair of green eyes, black hair, and fairies. That's one way to get to sleep.

THIS IS REAL

Wednesday 31st July 1822

Rachael sat again looking out of the window in the room she knew was her prison. The night had not changed her position. The day was sunny, and a light warm breeze drifted through the small gap she had created when she opened it last night. She hated stuffy places and hated to be confined. She laughed for a moment. Sitting behind a desk with her computer, typing away was never confining. Though she was sure many people would have thought it was. She had plenty of material for many a story now, despite having been in this time for a short period. Just over twenty-four hours and her life had been turned on its head.

She got up and began to pace around the room. She wanted to go downstairs but was worried the door would still be locked despite what Glenna had said last night. Besides, she had heard her lock it after she left. But someone had been in during the night. Clothes had been left for her on the chair.

Curiosity got the better of her and she went to the door and turned the handle. It opened.

Now what?

She stuck her head outside and saw one of the footmen. He bowed.

"I am to escort you down to breakfast Miss, when you're ready."

She smiled and closed the door. Leaning against the back of it she took in some short quick breathes. Seems Glenna was telling her the truth. She was free but was going to be watched very closely. Hence the waiting footman. She went over to the mirror and double checked her hair was in order. It was fine and so was her dress. The dress she had found was a beautiful light blue checked day dress. She was amazed how beautifully it fitted but also how she looked so comfortable in it.

Ominous.

She went out the door, smiled at the footman and asked him to deliver a message to the laird.

"Please tell him that I plan to stay in my room, as the prisoner he thinks that I am."

She stepped back into her room and closed the door. She heard the footsteps retreat from the door and then another pair come and position themselves outside her room.

Oh, he had everything in order.

But she had no intention of making it easy. He was going to make them work. Being alone for a while gave her a chance to think. And she had no desire to again be treated the way she had last night.

She walked to the chest of drawers to see what else may have been placed in her room as she slept. She was not disappointed. She found paper, a bottle of ink and a quill in the top draw. She had confided in Glenna about her passion to write and she was sure that they were here thanks to her newfound friendship. Strange that she did not see Glenna as the enemy.

She took them out and placed them on the table. She returned to the draws and continued her investigation. There were some of the clothes that she had tried on with Glenna yesterday. She assumed they had been altered and ready for her to use. There were underwear items that she would look forward to asking Glenna more about. Even some simple jewellery. She picked up the Celtic silver cross and placed it around her neck. She had always been fascinated by anything Celtic. It was a pleasure to wear it.

About ten minutes later Rachael had settled herself at the table and had begun to practice using the quill. She chuckled to herself as it caught on the paper. But she soon had the hang of it. She was hungry but did not want to sit in front of the gentlemen to be cross-examined again. Glenna would not allow her to go hungry. She was sure that after breakfast she would bring her something to eat. She could wait.

She heard the door open and braced herself.

Had Duncan come to fight?

No, it was Glenna and some maids. She moved her writing equipment from the table as the girls placed food and drinks on it. Glenna said nothing but sat down in the other chair waiting for the maids to finish. Another table was brought in and that too had items that indicated to Rachael that breakfast was going to take place in her room. She just hoped the men were not coming to join in.

"Well, don't stare at me like that. I won't let you starve, will I?"

The footman attempted to close the door after the maids exited.

"Leave the door open, MacGregor. We want some air to flow through here. I hate it when the air is stifled." She got up and opened the window wider.

"Let us have some breakfast while we plan what to do with the day."

Rachael laughed out loud. This woman will stare down her brothers whatever they decide to do. She had given her friendship and support to a stranger in one day. More than anyone had done for her ever before. She had not expected Glenna to boycott breakfast with the men, but she had and then had placed it fair and square in front of her.

"Come eat. We have much to talk about."

"You astound me, Glenna. Thank you."

"There is no need for thanks. Seeing my brother's bewildered faces was all the thanks that I needed. Come let us eat."

"That meal was wonderful. But I really did not expect you to come up here with all this. I just did not want to face another interrogation and argument with your brothers."

"That is exactly what I told Duncan. But he was convinced you were doing it out of spite."

Rachael smiled but spite was not on her mind. She had not slept well. Duncan had invaded her dreams a little too often, the previous night and placed her in some very unusual places. Nothing that she would reveal to Glenna. But she hoped her face would not reveal her thoughts.

"My brother will see you are not a danger to him or our family. He will come to terms with the real reasons you have found yourself here. It will take time and a bit of trust."

"You believe me then, that I come from the future?"

"Most definitely. The fae have a reason you must be here and now. I do not begin to understand why but yes, I do believe that you came from the future. Duncan will see that in time."

"I'm relieved that you believe in me but also amazed that you have befriended me, Glenna. I could be lying." She paused and looked at the hands that rested in her lap. Dreams could not have given her such a friend and she was so grateful for Glenna's support. "Thank you. There is no reason for you to believe but you do and I'm grateful."

"There is nothing to thank me for. You do not appear to be a liar and I am known for my ability to judge character, yes even at my age. I also felt that the fae were about to do something and well I believe you are that something. I want us to spend the day talking about lots of things. Your home, the future, your family and then perhaps we can think on why the fae have sent you."

Her smile helped Rachael breathe a little easier. In twenty-four hours, she had come to terms with her predicament and had found a friend who would support her as she came to terms with this new stage of her life.

Would she ever get back home?

That was up to the fae.

"I will have the maids clean this up and you and I shall go for a walk in the garden. The day is warm, and we can continue our conversation out in the world. I will tell you some of the family stories that make me believe you have to be from the future. Then you will know why it is easier for me to believe that you are here and that you are not lying."

Rachael and Glenna went downstairs following the maids after they had cleaned up their breakfast dishes. Rachael turned and saw the footman following them. She smiled at him as they went out the door leading to the garden. He was always within sight, watching them but kept away from the young ladies as they spoke together.

"These family legends you believe to be truth?"

"Most definitely. My mother passed many of them on to my father who in turn told them to me. My brothers showed no interest."

"But your mother was a Buchannan not a Murray, so how would she be aware of the Murray stories?"

Glenna pointed to a stone bench under one of the trees and they sat down.

"That is a very long story and I will share it with you but not today. The most important story I want to tell you are of three visitors who came to the hill."

Rachael leaned back on the trunk of the tree. "Would you be offended if I close my eyes while you tell me?"

"Of course not, but why?"

"As I told you earlier, I write, and I often close my eyes so that I can picture my stories. I would like to do that now while you tell me of the three visitors. I want to imagine what they look like."

"Very well. I will help you picture them by describing what they look like if I remember anything that was told to me. We have had many visitors to our hill. One was a doctor. But he was a doctor from the past. He could not believe that we lived in such a beautiful castle. He was scruffy they say, and some of the clan felt that he could not be a doctor. This was when my father was a boy. My father often said that he never liked being near the man. But one day my father fell from a tree and broke his arm. The man was there within a minute and carefully took my father to his room and examined his arm. He wrapped it and placed special herbs between the bandages along with pieces of straight wood from the tree that my father had fallen out of. My grandfather came to them and he could see that the stranger wanted to help. My grandfather allowed his ministrations but had his own doctor sent for. But our doctor could not fault his treatment. Needless to say, my father was healed and showed no ill effects from his accident."

Rachael could picture all the details of the incident in her mind. "I don't know what the stranger looked like, but I seem to be able to conjure up an image that suits. You will have to tell me what your father looked like so that I can picture him properly."

"That will be easy. Imagine the green eyes of Duncan and a taller version of him with red hair instead of black and you will have my father."

"Was your father really that similar to Duncan?"

"Oh yes, and their natures are similar too. My father did not want to be laird either and sometimes found his job difficult especially after my mother died. Duncan is a gentle man, but he carries too many cares on his shoulders. You are not seeing him as he truly is."

"I do find that hard to believe. I have only seen his anger."

"That will change. You have time, you will see."

Rachael smiled. Glenna was eighteen going on forty-eight. The woman had wisdom beyond her years.

"Then tell me of the second visitor." Rachael closed her eyes again.

"The second visitor was also a man who had come from the future, like you. This was in the 1700's. It was during the time of my great grandfather. He warned the clan to take care of all the families and feed them and put food away, food that they could use later. After Culloden, food was scarce, but our family survived because my ancestor paid attention and had done what the visitor had suggested."

"So, these visitors helped when they came. That's interesting. It's as if the fae knew that they would be needed. Perhaps then I might be able to be used to help you or your family."

"Ahhh, but that was not always the reason. Some did nothing and ran back to the hill and disappeared. Others just ran away. There is a story of one who could not make the family understand him. His language was not something anyone recognised. And after some months, he jumped from the tower."

"That's awful."

"Yes, but that is why we carry the stories forward and why my father took so much interest. My mother had a fascination for them, so he passed all these stories on to her, the ones that he was aware of. And some a written down in diaries and such." She paused. Rachael opened her eyes and then closed them again. Glenna continued.

"The third visitor involves my mother. But I will save that for another time. For now, I want you to tell me about your future life. What you have done, your family, your interests, and if there are any men in your future? This information will not be shared with my brothers. I have no intention in sharing anything with them. Trust me."

Rachael did.

The women involved themselves in deep conversation. Tea was served around them, under the tree as they continued their lengthy discussions. He wanted them to be comfortable. He was astounded to watch Rachael speak to his sister in such a relaxed way. He wanted to experience that. From the tower battlements, Duncan watched them converse. His sister would find out what he needed to know. But would she tell him? He doubted it.

"The hardest part is that I miss my conversations with both my mum and dad. They were my friends and not just my parents."

"I think I understand. As I grew, I watched my father spend more and more time with me. I reminded him of mother. It must have been so hard for him to not have his soul mate by his side." Rachael watched as Glenna lowered her eyes to her hands in her lap.

"Was their love that deep?"

"From all accounts, yes. My mother believed the stories and

wanted the clan to pass them on. Father had experienced its truth but seemed to have his own doubts about the truth of them. Until my mother arrived after they married. I have done my best to pass on the stories. Mother was a unique individual and he felt her loss greatly. He loved her till the day he died."

Rachael paused and turned her head to look out over the lawns gracing the front of the castle. She sighed and was suddenly homesick. The lush green of the Scottish Highlands was different to the rolling fields of wheat or canola that surrounded her farmhouse in Australia. She was enjoying the bond growing between her and Glenna, but she knew it was fleeting. She would have to return to her time, and soon. She could not stay here forever.

Rachael watched as a stylish Duncan walked purposefully towards them. The peace of the morning was about to be destroyed and she would not allow it. She stood as he came forward.

"I'm sorry to disturb your revelry. But I wanted to let you know that luncheon will be served soon."

Glenna also stood.

Rachael turned and spoke directly to Glenna. "I'm sorry but I believe I will return to my room." Before he had a chance to comment she bid a hasty retreat toward the castle.

"What did I say?" He turned and watched Rachael walk swiftly to the doors.

"She is hurting. She does not know why she has been sent here and you scare her. You're always angry."

"But I wasn't this time. I was on my best behaviour."

"I assume she did not want to give you the opportunity to yell at her again." Glenna faced him, her arms folded and her face revealing nothing.

"Glenna, please be careful, she could be a spy. What did she tell you? You were talking for so long and she was most animated."

"Ah, so you have been watching us. Well, there is nothing to tell you. If there is, she will tell you herself when she is ready. Now excuse me, but I plan to have luncheon with her in her prison."

Glenna headed toward the same doors that he had just watched Rachael enter. He had no fight left. He had lost the respect of his sister. He would never say that to Glenna, but he sensed it. His tempter had gotten the better of him. Things would have to change. He would have to change.

I NEED TO SEE A MAN ABOUT A DOG

F*riday 3rd August 1822*

Duncan had said little to either his sister or his brother since the morning in front of the castle. But he had watched. He had seen Rachael become familiar with her surroundings and retreat with any sign of him in her vicinity. He wanted things to change so had asked his sister to bring her to breakfast this morning. He was excited and somewhat terrified. He wanted to know more about her but was fearful what he might find out. He could no longer deny that he was attracted to her. He could not explain how he had become so enamoured of her, but he could no longer deny it. So, now he waited for her to arrive.

He could not take his eyes off her. Even Alasdair had noticed his constant observation of her movements and he did not like that piece of knowledge in his brother's hands.

"You really should get on with other matters, brother. After all, Glenna will tell us if there is anything of importance that she hears." He understood what his brother meant but he knew in his heart that Glenna would tell him nothing. Her nature was clear. She would not betray her new friend.

He had to convince them both that he had changed. Could he do it?

Rachael had agreed that life and her experiences would be better if she started taking part in the usual family activities. She had promised Glenna she would come down to breakfast this morning.

As she headed down the stairs, her footman was quietly following behind her. On the bottom floor she stopped and was unsure where to go next. The dining room or did they have a day room where breakfast was served. Her indecision must have shown. Her footman came up from behind her.

"Breakfast is usually served in the morning room, miss. If you will follow me." He bowed and headed down the same corridor she had walked the evening of her first dinner. But before they got to the dining room, they entered a corridor to the right. And finally, a room that was filled with light.

"Good morning, Rachael. I do hope you slept well." It was Glenna and she looked pleased to see her. Alasdair stood as she came toward the table. The footman pulled out the chair next to Glenna and she sat down.

"Good morning. I did sleep very soundly. Thank you." Duncan's image had been in her dreams again. Not that she would tell. But she had slept more soundly.

"I see you found the day dress I left in your room earlier."

"Yes. Thank you. It is beautiful and fits me like a glove." A breath of relief was released from her lungs. She looked around the table. She was amazed to see a blue and white Willow pearl ware settings in front of each of those partaking of breakfast. She tried to examine the markings without being too obvious and was amazed to see such a wonderful collection. She could also see that to the people around her it was just plain table ware but to her limited knowledge of antiques it was a wonderful sight. She smiled, knowing she knew the importance of this service to the future.

A plate of what appeared to be scrambled eggs and a smaller serving of fried potatoes was placed in front of her. She looked up at the footman and thanked him. He seemed surprised that she had spoken to him. She mentally chastised herself. They ignore servants in this time. She needed to be careful. Politeness was confined to the elite. Why should she follow their so-called manners? She chastised herself again. Well, she wanted to say thanks and was now glad that she had. She didn't care if they distrusted her any more than they already did. They don't trust her anyway so she would give them more to think about. She would be herself whether they liked it or not. The aromas drifting to her nose were enticing and she realised that she was *famished.* She partook and was delighted with the tastes that bombarded her mouth. After a moment she looked across at Alasdair.

"This food is delicious. Is Duncan, I mean the laird not having breakfast?" she asked.

"Ah. You will have to get up very early in the morning to have breakfast with the laird. He has had his hours ago. He deals with the farm manager, fixing any issues that may arise. He occasionally joins us here if he has certain jobs that he wants us to handle."

As if her saying his name was all she needed to do, Duncan appeared through the morning room door. The footman had just placed a cup of tea in front of her plate.

"I will have a tea also, MacGregor." He came over to the table and sat in the chair next to his brother. A moment later the footman who she knew was MacGregor, placed a cup of tea in front of the Laird.

"I do hope you slept well, Miss Fielding?" He sipped his tea.

"Why yes thank you...Sir." She lowered her head and continued to eat her breakfast. She did not want to look at him. She wanted to be polite but standoffish too if she could manage it.

"Please, call me Duncan." He sipped his tea again.

She finished her mouthful and raised her eyes to investigate those of Duncan. "Then call me Rachael." She could feel the heat rising to her face and neck. She lifted her hand to move her hair, that didn't need replacing. She lowered her eyes again. She did not appreciate being the bashful miss, but she would do it if it pleased her captor. Heck. *Why did she like this guy? He was a rude pig.* He meant nothing to her. He was not what she imagined the man in her painting would be like.

"I will. I assume that you would be happy to come with me into town. Just into Aberlour. I need to see a man about a dog."

Rachael started to laugh. She put down her cutlery and lifted her napkin to her lips. She was unable to cease the giggles emerging from her mouth.

"I dunna believe it is a laughing matter."

Duncan looked upset. She just could not help laughing. "I do apologise. It is just a joke where I come from..."

"Well," he paused, "It is not a joke to us, Miss Fielding. We are having problems with foxes getting in the hen house..."

She began to laugh again. "I am truly sorry but what you just said is so typical in the movies."

Everyone was staring at her but said nothing more. She pulled herself together.

"Sorry." She gave a sheepish grin to Glenna who was also finding it hard to control her mirth.

"This is not a laughing matter." He stood. "Miss Fielding, please be ready to accompany me in thirty minutes." He picked up his cup and quickly swallowed what was left of his tea and left the room. She watched him go and mentally kicked herself for allowing her sick sense of humour to get the better of her. The rough and angry Duncan was back.

She continued to eat her breakfast but was disconcerted to say the least. She still had to suppress the giggles wanting to come out.

"What is a movie?" Glenna asked.

"I really don't think that I should say much about the future. I might be creating some kind of paradox or something." She looked down at her food.

She could feel the eyes of Glenna and Alasdair burrowing into her head waiting for her to open her silly little mouth again. She restrained herself from seeing if she was right.

"Paradox. The girl is insane." Alasdair stood and threw his napkin on the table and left the room.

She was right.

Glenna had found for her a dark blue pelisse that she placed over her checked dress. It fitted her very well. Everything she had been given was of good quality and wonderfully comfortable. It was if Glenna had a wardrobe full of clothing made especially for her. She also wore a sun hat decorated with small blue flowers, matching her dress to perfection. She and Glenna were waiting in the foyer of the regency extension for Duncan to arrive. Was she really leaving the house? Leaving her room? And with him of all people. But she had lost her anger and wanted to get to know the family better. And yes, Duncan was high on the list of things she wished to understand.

"Why would he want me to go to town with him? I know what the place looks like. Well at least what it will look like." She gave her head a little shake." It was starting to ache again. "After all, he was yelling at me a few nights ago. Now, all is well? I don't think so."

"As I told you earlier, I believe that my brother is looking for proof for your story or proof that you have other reasons for being here. Just relax and enjoy the trip. Be yourself. That will confuse him enough." Glenna seemed extremely calm. She only wished it would rub off on her.

The quiet was soon overtaken by the sounds of boots coming down the pink granite stairway. Rachael turned to see Duncan. She had hoped to see him descend the stairs in some sort of highland dress. Why, she did not know. But he was in typical regency day clothes. She was slightly disappointed. Which was crazy because how often did she see a man in regency dress? He was so handsome. His tailcoat was a deep dark blue. That made his green eyes stand out. The beige full trouser went over what she believed to be ankle high black boots. His waist coat was light blue and neck cloth was beautifully tied. He was stunning. There was no other word for it. She stood there staring at a man who could easily take her breath away in her time and had in the here and now.

"Miss Fielding, you're looking beautiful in your pelisse. That dark blue goes so well with your eyes."

Rachael stood there with her mouth open. She could not believe that she had heard him correctly. He had paid her a compliment. It was the last thing she expected. There was no malice or contempt displayed in his eyes either.

He came over and lifted her chin so that her mouth closed. She could feel the heat rush to her cheeks.

"I do know how to compliment those who are beautiful. You need not be that dumbfounded." He put on his riding gloves as she continued to stare at him. Mouth tightly closed.

Okay. Her heart was beating at a hundred miles an hour. When he stood that close to her, she could almost hear his heart beating. She smiled and lowered her gaze. It was her heart that she could hear not his.

Get a grip.

He was not staring at her the way she had been staring at him.

Thank God that he wasn't, or things could get a little crazy.

Her expression changed. What had changed? He was happy and cheerful. None of the frowns or negativity that had been surrounding him every time she had been in his presence. He was all politeness and contentment. He was either a great actor or he might believe her story. Time would tell. Yes time. She did not have that long.

"Now Miss Rachael, let us have an enjoyable morning together while I discuss dogs with my associate."

That brought a smile to her face. Dogs: he had to see a man about a dog. She looked up into his face. He was smiling at her anticipating her next response. Then they locked gazes and she ran through the forest green depths that returned the gaze to hers.

"Can I suggest that you take Rachael for lunch at the Inn?"

Thank heavens that Glenna was there. She might have thrown herself into his arms. She had to stop thinking and acting like a schoolgirl. Yes, he was the man in the picture that she loved but he was still a man. She could handle this. She gave her head another shake.

"That is a wonderful idea, sister. Don't expect us back for luncheon."

"That is not necessary…"

"It is no problem at all. We will see the town and I will be interested to hear if it is similar in your time."

That got her attention. Rachael looked at Glenna who nodded and smiled.

He offered his arm to her and she placed her hand on his sleeve. She immediately felt the jolt that went through her. He must have also as he immediately looked down into her face as she stared up at him. They stared into each other's eyes. She saw hope, desire, and excitement. Then and there she hoped that one day she could meet the fairy that had sent her here so that she could thank them for this glorious experience. Examining his eyes and his inner being. She was in a time she loved. But she knew it wouldn't last. Those things she saw were not there. It was her imagination.

She was a witch, remember? He didn't trust her, remember?

They went out the front door and waiting for them was a neat and sturdy curricle. It was obviously built for the country rather than for showing off in London or Edinburgh. It was a very practical machine. He helped her up into the seat and then went around to climb in on the other side. After his master's signal the stable boy let go of the horse and they were off.

In moments they were out of the castle precinct and heading south toward the Fairy Hill and Aberlour. The day was cloudy, but rain did not figure in their movements. She hoped it would remain dry for the remainder of her little trip. The lightly ribboned bonnet that Glenna had given her to wear surprisingly helped to keep the sun from shining on her face. The air was crisp and clean. Rain had fallen during the night she could see from the occasional puddles. But it had not been heavy enough to create issues for the road.

"Thank you for coming with me today, Miss Fielding." The curricle gently bounced along.

"Can you call me Rachael? I'm not used to being called Miss Fielding. I even introduce myself as Rachael to my clients." She smiled up at him. She noticed the curious look he gave her.

"Very well, I will. Thank you. Will you call me Duncan?" He seemed hesitant. "I'm usually called Laird when I'm out and about. I would much rather be Duncan again." His gaze had taken him to a place that she could not see. Interesting.

"I assume that they call you that because you are the Laird. I know enough of this time to know that the way you addressed your superiors was very important." He smiled at her.

"I took over when my father died. It was not my plan." He paused and then changed the subject.

"Enough of me. What about you. Where are your parents?"

Drat.

She has started to get him to open a little and relax but just like that it was gone. She could sense that although he was not his usual angry self, he was still very keen to get what information he could get from her. There was still no trust. She looked at him briefly then responded.

"My parents are both dead. They died about...they died a while ago." She was having trouble telling him the truth. She knew that he would think her a liar. And telling the truth seemed to get her into trouble. Yet, she wanted him to be truthful. If he wanted to see the real her, she would try to say what she could. "They died in a car accident."

"A car accident? Do you mean a cart or carriage accident?"

"No Duncan, a car. It is a mechanical vehicle that you can drive around in much the same way that we are doing now. But with no horses. It is all mechanical."

"I see." He smiled again at her.

"No Duncan, you don't see. I promise to tell you the truth from now on. It's a problem though because there will be some things that I reveal you will know nothing about. All I ask is that you question me with an open mind and heart. And then determine if you think that I am telling you lies. In other words, don't just assume that I am lying or have a great imagination." She could see that he heard her but the look on his face convinced her that he did not want to understand what she really meant. How could he? He would always think her a liar. She lowered her eyes.

"Very well, Rachael. I see from the look on your face that you are telling me the truth. At least the truth as you perceive it."

She sighed. She looked at the green hills around her with the occasional hint of browning bracken. The smell. Oh, how she wanted to smell that country scent for the rest of her life. Crisp clean. Little hints of floral and earthy tones. The occasional waft of horse or of sandalwood. Yes, sandalwood from the man who sat next to her. That was probably as good as it would get around here. At least her senses could enjoy this unique experience.

She gazed briefly at him then back at the scenery. But his portrait, her painting continued to come into her vision. Beyond hope she wanted him to accept her. She knew his image. Knew him. But she so wanted him to be what she had always imagined. Her hero. Dreams. She was dreaming. They continued for the next few miles in silence.

The curricle turned onto the main road leading into Aberlour. It circled a large hill and came into the village from the south. Fairy Hill was up to his right looking over the village. Had she noticed? She had been too quiet since she announced that she was going to tell him the truth. He wanted to be sure she knew he was still in a friendly mood. Though he was finding it hard. Pretending to believe something that is not real can be difficult. Especially when he could see how sincere she really was.

Cars? Honestly?

"To your left is the remains of the old church. When Grant rebuilt the village, the old church was closed and the new one built over there." He pointed toward the small steeple of the new church. He watched as Rachael stared openly at the old church.

"There is only a little bit of wall left of the old church, in my time. But they really look after it."

He continued. "The street we are on is called..."

"High Street. It still is. But there are extra streets behind High street on both sides. But not now. There appears to be alley ways."

She was wide eyed, and her head darted from one side of the road to the other. She did honestly seem to recognise some of the buildings. Well, they had found her on the Fairy Hill, so she probably came up from the town.

Do not get drawn into her fantasy.

"That building is still there but dramatically altered. Oh, and then that building. It looks identical to what it looks like in the future. They must have really looked after it. Even the window frames are still white."

The more she pointed and commented on the buildings as they slowly made their way down the street, the more disconcerted he was. She really believed the things she was saying. But she could hold a normal conversation. She did not appear to be mad.

He pulled in under the arch of the old inn. The stable boy came out to take the reins from him. He got down from the curricle and came around to Rachael's side and helped her down. She smiled at him and she seemed to be happy. He was totally bewildered, but returned the smile hoping to calm her. They went into the inn.

"Good morning, Lord Murray. It is nice to have you call."

"Good morning, Crombie. Is the private room ready?"

"It is your lordship. Please come this way." He turned and walked down the hall and took them into a room on the right. There a small fire was lit though the weather was not cold. The drive in had been cooler than she had expected, and the day was cloudy. So the fire was a welcoming sight. Rachael undid the buttons of her pelisse and he helped her take it off. She had been glad of it on the curricle ride. He had not yet removed his coat. She also took off her hat.

"If you would wait here, I will go find the man I wish to talk to, and we will return here. I will return as soon as I can."

"Very well." She replied but he could see the suspicion in her eyes. Perhaps she had sensed he was testing her.

It was so obvious to her that she was placed here in this room, alone, as a test. Would she run away and prove to him that she had been lying all along? She knew she wasn't far from Fairy Hill, but the time of day was all wrong if Glenna's story was to be believed. She was not going to pass this test. He wouldn't trap her that easily. She had to make him see the truth. She couldn't explain why it was so important to her but nothing else seemed to matter. The brief glimpse of his smiles this morning had stirred something in her heart. Besides, it was a longish walk to Fairy Hill from here and she really didn't think these shoes would last half a mile let alone up the hill.

Crombie entered the room. "Can I get you something to drink, ma'am?"

"Crombie, is it? Would it be possible to have a small pot of tea and something light to eat?"

"Yes ma'am." He turned to leave.

"Oh, and Crombie? Could I have...a news sheet if you have it?" She smiled sweetly at him.

He looked a little surprised. Perhaps women were not big readers of the papers. He bowed and turned to leave the room.

"Thank you, Crombie. I appreciate it."

He turned back to her and smiled, bowed, then left the room.

A few minutes later he came in with a small pile of papers. By then she had seated herself near the window. It looked out toward the river. The river she loved, the Spey. She thanked him and she went to work reading what he'd left, wanting to keep her mind off the fact that she was being tested. She knew. She had seen one of Duncan's footmen, admittedly in ordinary clothing outside the main door of the inn. Did he think her stupid? That she would not recognise something or someone that obvious? After all she had gotten to know all the footman who had been watching her for the last few days. A few minutes later, tea and scones were brought in.

There was a great cross section of news sheets from all over the country. As this was an inn where travellers stopped, she should have known there would be. Many were some weeks or months out of date, but she was fascinated to read the information they held. There was an Inverness Courier, Aberdeen Journal, and an Edinburgh Advertiser. But further flung papers such as the Dublin Evening Post, which was three months out of date and two different copies, both London Courier and Evening Gazette.

She settled back on the lounge and started to absorb all that she could. She chuckled. No one would believe that she could get her hands on such great research material.

———

"Has she tried to leave the building?" Duncan was terrified that the answer would prove him right. That she had lied and was just looking for a way to escape his continual questioning.

"No, your lordship. She ordered some tea and some reading material and has not moved since you left her."

That had been almost an hour. His footmen were positioned around the building and all had told him the same thing. She was still inside.

"She has been reading old news sheets, your lordship. She has had tea and scones and I have heard her laughing out loud on occasions but that has been the total extent of her activity."

"Thank you, Crombie." He could not believe that she had not moved. "Mr Slessor of Aberdeen should be arriving shortly. Please bring him in when he arrives. Oh, and can you supply us with more tea and scones please?"

"Yes, your lordship."

———

She was engrossed in her reading when Duncan returned.

"I see you have been busy since I left you."

"Oh, Duncan this has been wonderful. To read events that I saw but as history."

He was taken aback by her passion and excitement. He had been trying to trap her but instead she was absorbing the information of this time. That is if he believed what she was saying. He did not.

"Oh. That is interesting. My visitor, Mr Slessor should be arriving at any time. I would rather you did not mention where you have come from. Just say you are visiting from London."

She started to gather the papers around her. "Did you want me to wait in another room?" She seemed a little upset.

"No. You're welcome to hear the discussion about the dog." He smiled and she beamed back at him. He went over and picked up one of the news sheets. "I have many old papers at the castle if you would like to examine them."

"That would be wonderful. This one," she picked up the most recent copy of the Edinburgh Advertiser, "says that the dates have been finalised and that the king will be in Edinburgh on 14th of August. That is only a week away. Are you planning to go?"

"All the lairds have been summoned by Scott and the King."

"That's funny. I mean peculiar, that you placed Scott before the king?"

"Not as far as I am concerned. Scott has been organising everything. The man has been obsessed. He is a total romantic and has lost all sense of what the real history of Scotland is about. I would not leave him in charge of organising a country dance. But the king gave him that honour. And you cannot disagree with the king. Scott is ridiculous." The angry Duncan was back, and he was sure she noticed. She gave him a timid smile.

"Sir Walter Scott is revered in my time as the man who helped to redefine Scotland into the wonderful nation that it is today. Well, what it will be. And it is in my time. I love visiting Scotland." Her eyes drifted to the window and he could see her thoughts were elsewhere.

"Scotland has always been a great nation. We do not need the lackeys, the newly bayonetted puppets of the king nor do we need the King of England, to define us. We are who we are. You English..."

"Please stop yelling at me, and I am not English."

He was taken aback. He had not realised that he had raised his voice. He knew his temper always got the better of him when it came to Scotland. He looked at his hands balled into fists by his side and released them. He did not want to scare her. He smiled at the lady sitting stock still in front of him. She continued.

"Duncan, Scotland is great and always has been in my eyes and heart. You have to believe me."

"I apologise. When it comes to my homeland, my Scotland..."

"You don't want anyone messing with it."

"As you say." He was perturbed. Her language was strange but accurate in its simplicity. It was a messy situation, being under the English King and authority. He did not like it being tampered with. His image of Scotland was true. He did not want it 'messed' with by Scott or anyone else. He realised she could see exactly who he was and how he thought. Now he was uncomfortable.

"Certain things upset me. I apologise."

"You need not be upset. Scotland is great and always will be."

But he had no chance to pursue her comment any further as Crombie entered the room and introduced Mr Slessor and his dog.

WE HAD A LOVELY DAY AND THEN...

The ride back was more relaxed. Rachael observed how much more relaxed they were in each other's company. They had connected. Having spent the day discovering more about each other was more than she had expected. Duncan had not said anything that would confirm what she was thinking. But things seemed right. But that is what she wanted to believe. Perhaps he was starting to trust her. There had been the occasional moments of silence but they were comfortable in each other's company. When they did speak, they were sharing thoughts and ideas that challenged them both.

The sun was shining, the clouds having dissipated, as the curricle slowly made its way home. He did not seem to be in a rush as he had been this morning. She noticed dark clouds seemingly building in the west. She sat quietly and went over the events of the morning, enjoying the ride back to the castle.

Being in the same room with this man was a challenge. Watching him negotiate the purchase of a hound was beyond anything she had ever hoped to witness. Through the whole interview, the dog sat straight and tall. That was until she had summoned it to her, and he rested his head on her lap for the remainder of the interview. The hound had deposited himself at her feet as they enjoyed the wonderful lunch the inn had provided. It now sat soundly asleep on the seat of the curricle and half on her lap. She smiled to herself. Duncan had seen a man about a dog.

"Can I ask you why you are smiling?" Duncan looked at her with an open welcoming expression.

"I'm smiling that you did actually see a man about a dog. Where I come from, you say that when you don't want someone to know where you are going. Or you don't want them to know your business."

Duncan looked at her and shook his head. She detected a frown. But he said nothing.

"That is the truth, Duncan. I said that I would tell you the truth." She waited patiently for him to say something. But the minutes dragged on. She kept her head down and remained silent... Why did she dream that he would believe her? The dog lifted his head and licked the tears from her face. She held him closer. She hadn't realised that she had been crying. She didn't want Duncan to see. She didn't say another word and neither did Duncan.

The curricle pulled up in front of the doors of the castle. Rachael slowly lifted the dog's head off her lap and jumped down from the curricle leaving the dog sitting on the seat. She didn't wait for him to help her down. The dog jumped off and followed Rachael into the house. Why had he not said something to her? He knew that she was crying despite her efforts to conceal it from him. As she ran into the house, he wanted to call out to her to say that he believed her. But he couldn't because he did not want to believe that the woman who spoke with a peculiar accent and knew things that he was sure she had made up, might actually be telling him the truth.

He handed the reins to the groom who led the curricle away toward the stables. He stood there looking at the door of the castle waiting for Rachael to return and stand in front of him. Of course, she did not. He was not sure how long he stood there but suddenly his sister Glenna stood in front of him, her hands on her hips. She was angry and he had no doubt why she was.

"Don't say a word. I know." He just looked at her.

"If you know why, then tell me what kind of man, no, fool, makes a woman cry? She is in such anguish and pain. What in the name of the fae did you say?"

"I didn't say anything. That is why she is upset. I'm sorry."

His sister let her arms drop to her sides and said nothing. The shocked look on her face, hearing him concede to her must have taken her fight away. Her mouth was open, but she said nothing. He lifted his hand, placed his finger under her chin and closed her mouth. "Yes, I'm sorry. I will talk to her when I know what to say. Right now, I need to be alone, to think. She is so sure that what she has told me is the truth." With that he went past his sister and into the castle to head to his study and to a bottle of whisky he knew would be waiting for him. He noticed the dark clouds from the west had closed in around the castle. The sweet smell of a storm was in the air both inside and outside.

Why on earth had he remained quiet? It was obvious to even him that she had hoped he would reply in a positive manner. But he had not. He had observed her closely through the morning. He had never seen a cultured young lady take to a hound as she had. She loved paying the dog attention and the dog loved her undivided pampering. He closed the door to his study and went to the sideboard to pour himself a drink. He sat behind his desk and now asked the most dangerous of questions. Did he believe her? Was she from the future? Away from her he could easily deny her ranting and stories. But while with her he could not deny that she believed what she was saying. She was telling him the truth. Would he believe? How could he?

While pondering how to fix the current situation he now found himself in, he saw Alasdair enter the study. His brother stood for a moment looking at him.

"Glenna is not happy that you upset her new friend." He went to the sideboard and poured himself a drink and sat in the chair opposite his desk. "She is bewildered as to how you have ruined such a day."

"I understand her confusion. The day has not gone the way that I had thought it might." He looked across at Alasdair. "She never made any attempt to escape let alone try to deviate me to the Hill. She was all politeness and totally enamoured with the things that I was doing. She asked many questions but none that would indicate she had some kind of motive to trap or trick me. Most related to her version of the future that she insists she comes from." He placed the glass on the desk and lowered his feet to the floor, pulling the chair in toward the desk. "Truthfully, I rather enjoyed her company."

"Then dear brother, what on earth did you do to upset her?"

"It's simple. I did not acknowledge that she was telling the truth. She honestly seemed hurt and I do not know, heartbroken, that I did not participate in the lie. Trouble is that my head says don't believe a word she says but my heart says she tells the truth."

"Ahh."

"What does that mean?"

Alasdair leaned forward. "It would seem, that she has made a deeper impression on you than we had planned. Remember we were going to pretend that she was telling the truth. But now you tell me you believe her. That does not bode well."

"I'm not sure that I believe her but there are things that she says and the way she behaves that make...I don't know. Perhaps I'm the one who is going mad."

Alasdair leaned back into the chair. "Well, what do we do now? Do we continue to pretend or believe her to be telling the truth?"

Taking a deep breath Duncan leaned back and let his sigh come from deep within his chest. Plans be damned. He wanted the truth. He paused and then smiled at his brother.

"I have it. We will assume she is telling the truth. Let us go to our aunt's house in Edinburgh. There, or on the way, we should be able to glean more from her. We will be confined in the carriage with her, after all. We will not hurry but take days to get there. Stopping in various places for meals and to change horses. Have a relaxed trip to town."

Alasdair leant forward. Duncan paused to see his brother's interest, then continued.

"We'll watch to see again if she tries to get away or reveals her real motives of being on Fairy Hill. We need to be in Edinburgh soon so that I can deal with the king's visit." He was sure that his brother would not think it wise to take her, but he really wanted to see if she had any connection to the king. This way he could watch her even more closely and wait to see whom she recognised or communed with.

Alasdair added, "I will ride, and we can take turns in and out of the carriage. We do not want her to feel desperate, confined with both of us watching her. If we surround her too much she may panic. Someone might get hurt. That is if she is doing something that is underhanded."

"Agreed. We'll leave after an early breakfast in the morning." Duncan got up and went to the bell pull. "I will inform Glenna and have her tell our visitor over dinner. We can watch her reaction."

"I do not know what my brother is thinking. I wish I did. But we need to leave for Edinburgh, says my brother, in time to see the king." She watched as Glenna paced back and forth in front of her. The storm had hit a few minutes ago but the tension that she had earlier seemed to dissipate with the rain. She was angry at herself for letting Duncan affect her so. Glenna's tension was a great diversion for her.

"But Glenna, I only have a few clothes that you have loaned to me. How on earth will I survive the king's visit? Mind you it would be wonderful to meet someone like him from history, if you know what I mean?"

Glenna smiled. Rachael knew that she was revealing her concern to her friend.

Glenna took her hand and gave it a squeeze. "I have many clothes and I am sure Duncan will purchase what evening wear you will need."

"He might just lock me up in your house and throw away the key. Why would he even let me near Edinburgh if he dislikes me so much, let alone not trust me? He does not believe me despite my being totally upfront and truthful with him today. I think that he is even more suspicious of me than he was before."

Glenna moved in and took her into her arms and hugged her. Rachael thought of her friend Sam and how she often would hug her when she was feeling low. She lifted her hands and hugged Glenna back. She missed Sam but Glenna was a new friend who would help her if she asked for it. And that was reassuring.

"Thank you for believing in me, Glenna. I appreciate that more than you will know."

"Tis not hard, my friend, to believe in the truth." She pulled away from her, smiling and continued, "We must dress now for dinner and then we will pack, for I believe we will be leaving early in the morning for Edinburgh. My brother has said we will. But he did not want me to tell you. He wanted to witness your reaction over dinner. He will not allow me to ride, which would be quicker, so we will be going by carriage. And if that is the case, we need to leave very soon. Now, do not forget, just be yourself over dinner. I have no intention of playing his silly games. So, react to us leaving as you wish. Come down for dinner when you have dressed."

Glenna left the room and she was again alone. What a day. She had done all she could to tell the truth to Duncan and he still did not believe her. But then, why should he? She hardly could believe that she was in the past, but she was and needed to keep that in mind. She would go to Edinburgh and enjoy the visit and the history that she would witness. But when they got home, well back here to the castle at least, she would have to get back to Fairy Hill and her own time. She turned and looked at the beautiful rich red dress on her bed. And then looked to heaven and thanked Glenna's father who had spoilt the girl.

Rachael came into the dining room. Both gentlemen stood and bowed to her. Duncan pulled the seat out next to him. Glenna was already seated next to Alasdair. Well, at least she didn't have to look into Duncan's face. She sat down and kept her head down to avoid looking into those green eyes. She could almost feel the warmth radiating from his body as he was now so close to her.

Her imagination was going to get her in trouble one day.

"Ah Miss Rachael, that delectable redcurrant dress makes you look good enough to eat." Alasdair was still trying to pitch himself to her. Heck, she was crazy to have fallen for Josh. Josh and Alasdair were so much alike. She did not acknowledge the man's comment.

"Don't be ridiculous brother, it would be such a waste of a

perfectly good dress." Glenna giggled.

"I thank you sir, but I would agree with your sister." She did not look to him. This guy needed no encouragement.

Alasdair gave a hearty laugh.

"My brother, despite his metaphor, is correct. You do look wonderful."

She lifted her head and smiled directly at Duncan. Her stomach did a summersault as the dark deep green eyes stared at her. My God, he was gorgeous. His unfinished portrait flashed into her mind. He continued to pierce her with his stare.

"We plan to leave for Edinburgh in the morning. The servants will help you pack what you need. My sister will give you what she can, and I will make sure that you have what extra you might need when we get to the city." *Well, Glenna was correct. They were going.*

As he spoke, she did not take her eyes from him. She could neither react with shock or with excitement. The thought of days with him travelling to Edinburgh warmed her. Even though she knew he neither cared for her nor believed that she was telling him the truth. But the coming days would put them very close together and she was not opposed. She wanted to get to know her portrait, well at least the man whom she had admired for so long. So far what she had imagined she had not seen. Her image was very different in personality.

"I appreciate greatly the chance to experience this wonderful piece of history." The corner of his mouth lifted ever so slightly but his eyes were smiling. She turned to look at Glenna who was grinning from ear to ear. Perhaps she had won him over after all. Though he made no mention of the events at the end of their day that had upset her so. If only he believed in her. She wanted that more than she could understand why.

She looked at Alasdair. He was grinning. She did not return a smile. Instead, she looked back into the green eyes that had captivated her. The eyes of Duncan. And she smiled at him.

LEAVING FOR EDINBURGH

Thursday 8th August 1822

It was still dark when she dressed for the day. The evening before Glenna and she had sorted and tried on many dresses, pelisses as well as bonnets. The maids had made the adjustments all night so that they would be ready for her when she left. Glenna was extremely generous in what she would let her wear. She even had a travel cloak for her to use. The servants arranged their luggage, and most were taken downstairs to be loaded in the cart that would leave before them, first thing in the morning. She was now excited at the prospect of seeing the countryside she had recently travelled through but now she was back in its history. Would it look the same? She knew that modernity would not be present but the excitement of comparing them did not escape her.

Glenna knocked at her door and they made their way down for breakfast. The gentlemen were already seated and enjoying the early start. She gathered some eggs and a little toast from the sideboard and sat at the table next to Glenna. The gentlemen were seated in front of them.

"I must say that the thought of travelling by carriage to Edinburgh excites me." She smiled at the men. "I have never travelled by carriage before." Their faces showed signs of doubt at her comment, but they held their tongues.

It was Glenna who broke the silence as they quietly ate.

"The roads are not too bad and the small amount of rain we had last night should not hinder us much. The storm did not last very long, did it, Duncan?"

Duncan lifted his head and smiled at his sister. "No, my dear, it did not."

Rachael knew they were not really talking about the weather. She smiled then gave her head a little shake and decided to change the topic of conversation.

"How long will it take? Should we be there by tomorrow?" They all looked at Rachael as if she had just fallen from the sky. It didn't take her long to get here when she drove up.

"Not even if we travelled all night, which we will not be doing." Came the calm but serious voice of Duncan. "We will arrive in Edinburgh in four days."

"Four days? You are kidding? It's only about one hundred and sixty miles."

Duncan rose to his feet. He looked at her and smiled.

"I am not sure how fast you travel where you come from, madam, but I wish to rest our horses and ourselves as we travel along. I have horses waiting for us at Aviemore, Blair Athol and Perth. I do not want to press them. I will also not travel at night. It is not safe to do so. Besides, it will give us all a lovely chance to see the country." With that he bowed and went to the door. He turned, "and we will leave within the hour. I want luncheon at Cromdale." He looked directly at her. "I want to see a man about a dog." He smiled and left the room.

That was not what she had expected. He was joking with her of course, except for the travel. Four days seemed a long time to be getting to Edinburgh but then she was going to be travelling the same route that she took in her future. The northern road into the highlands. Now she could compare. A tingle went up her spine. This was going to be exciting.

They were soon on their way. A cart with most of their luggage had already left and would meet the party in Aviemore some 35 miles away. The drive was delightful and the weather glorious. Scotland would often show all four seasons in one day but so far, the day was warmish and dry. Glenna had been correct. The small amount of rain they had had the night before did not interfere with their travelling.

Duncan road his horse, a beautiful black stallion. He held his seat and sat tall and straight. Occasionally he would gallop ahead and give his horse legs to move. But he was always close. The road seemed busy to her. But she had nothing to compare it too. In her time cars moved rather more quickly. She had made the comment and Alasdair agreed.

"Perhaps others were on their way for the king's visit." He said. And she had to agree. The bulk of the traffic was heading south toward the city.

"Perhaps." She replied. "I guess the king coming to Scotland is a big thing. In years to come many in the royal family will love visiting Scotland." He looked at her and smiled but she could see the doubt in his eyes. It would take a lot to convince him and Duncan that she was telling the truth. She wanted to tell them of Victoria and Albert, her German prince who loved Scotland more than any other. Enough to build a castle for his queen. Of the minibus tour she took that went through the lands of Balmoral.

And a Queen who drove her own land rover that she had witnessed from the minibus window.

Having Glenna in the carriage with her gave her comfort. She really didn't want to be in it alone with Alasdair. She, of course, had studied carriages for the books she wrote but had never ridden in one. It was rougher than she expected but assumed that was due to the road rather than the vehicle. Overall, it was comfortable. It was in good condition and seemed sturdier than a town carriage. The leather seats were well padded and clean and the adornments appropriate for a well to do family. She had seen many of them in museums in London and other parts of England. As they lived so far from Edinburgh, that made sense to her that they would have a sturdy vehicle that could do the travelling that was required between the highlands and town.

They had been travelling for a few hours when they stopped briefly at Advie to allow the horses to drink. They all took the moment to stretch their legs. Travelling through these green valleys was magical and Rachael could believe in fairies as she looked around. This whole environment could conjure up a fairy easily. Fairies, gnomes and even giants. The fables and fairy tales could easily be based on truth, as she looked at the scenery that surrounded her. More so than any other place on earth.

She looked at the road ahead and could see the Cairngorms rising ahead of them. She knew the road skirted around them in the future and assumed the road ahead would do the same. She wished she had her camera. But then how would she explain that piece of science?

Glenna came and stood beside her.

"I am amazed at how little of the landscape has changed. Sure, there are less people and towns are smaller, but the country looks as beautiful in the future as it does now."

"Ahh, that does not surprise me. Scotland has been and always will be beautiful. It is a prized possession. That is why the Scottish are so possessive."

Rachael nodded. She knew a man that fitted that description exceedingly well.

"Why is it, Glenna, that you just accept everything I say?"

"Because my dear, I can tell who says the truth and who knows it to be so and those who would pretend." Just then Alasdair came and stood beside them. This was disconcerting. She wanted to flesh out more of what Glenna was saying but Alasdair would not allow that. Surprisingly, he did it for her without realising it.

"Well, if you know that sister why do you not marry one of the men that are in love with you?"

"Quite easily Dair, none of them love me. They love my money more. Besides, I am only eighteen and still have plenty of time." She took Rachael's arm and they walked to the other side of the carriage. There they found Duncan watering his horse.

"We will be leaving shortly," he told them as they came to stand near him. "We will be in Cromdale in time for luncheon. The horses can have a real rest and so will we. I have reserved a room for you ladies to freshen up and rest if you desire. And another room where we can have refreshments together." His eyes were fixed on her and she smiled.

"That would be wonderful," was all she could say. Alasdair came around and took the reins off his brother.

"You travel with the ladies. I need to ride." He got on the horse and road away at a gallop.

"Well ladies. It would seem that you have frightened him off. Do I need to fear escorting you in the carriage?" The ladies chuckled and walked toward the carriage door. The footman came and opened it, then helped Glenna to climb in.

Duncan took her by the hand and led her to the carriage door as the driver mounted the front of the carriage. She got in and sat opposite Glenna and was quickly followed by Duncan who sat next to his sister. Probably so that he could keep his eyes on her. Did he think that she would jump out of a moving carriage? Was that what he was thinking? The heat went to her face and she was sure he knew. He smiled knowingly. He knew she was uncomfortable.

The jerk.

Why did she let him tease her?

They rode on. The air was cooler as they rose into the foothills. The travelling cloak came in handy and she was glad of it as she wrapped it around her shoulders. The sky was still blue and had but a scattering of clouds. Everything here was so lush and green. Bracken was beginning to turn to brown but only in places that had experienced an early frost. After all it was still late summer. Oh, how she loved this country.

The trip to Cromdale was wonderful. Duncan discussed the history of the area, how many of the clans had battled over the centuries to lay claim to these highland mountains. Rachael was enthralled with everything he said, and she did not hide her excitement. He mentioned some of the folktales common to the area and she watched as Glenna drew closer to her brother and was soon snuggling into his shoulder. Within minutes she was asleep with her brother stroking her hair. For a short time, they remained quiet as Glenna slept.

Rachael looked at the tender moment as the scenery floated by. She then looked out over the glorious countryside.

"It is clear to me, Miss Rachael, that you love Scotland as you have said. You have been so enamoured with the scenery that we have been driving through this day."

"I am, but just call me Rachael. I love that the scenes around me seem so familiar but just a little different. That was not what I expected. It makes me realise that Scotland has always been beautiful and rugged. Not so 'handled' by people."

"You really believe you're from the future, don't you?"

She took in a deep breath and quietly whispered, so as not to wake Glenna. "Duncan, I said that I would only tell you the truth so yes, that is what I believe. I have no other explanation. And no other reason to be here." She remained quiet as she watched Duncan in contemplation. She wanted him to believe her more than anything that she had ever wanted. She didn't know why but she wanted it.

"Very well. I will too, for now."

"No Duncan you either do or you don't." She stared at him hoping that he could see that she was serious. She did not want any more pretence. Just the truth.

"Then I believe you, most sincerely."

She observed him for a moment then smiled. "Good, about time too."

"Tell me, does the countryside look the same in future? Are there not improvements?"

She had to believe him and happily told him of her drive from Edinburgh to Aberlour. In the future. And the differences that existed.

He listened to her intently. He was glad that Glenna slept so that he could seek out more responses from Rachael. After all he did not want his sister to think that he really did believe that the fairies were active in Scotland.

"There are distilleries all over this stretch of road. The tourists come from everywhere to sample the great Scottish drink."

He could not deny that she really believed she was from the future. The woman was not mad. She was intelligent but clearly confused as to how she got to Fairy Hill. His sister trusted her, and Glenna had always been able to tell the *highland cows from the sheep*. He chuckled to himself. She had turned down several of his gentlemen friends and he could not blame her.

"What is a tourist?" he asked.

"They are people from all around the world who come and visit Scotland in my time. I was one of them. My family brought me here when I was a teenager."

"A teenager?"

"A young adult. In my time, Glenna would be a teenager. Perhaps I should not say any more. I don't want to upset the way things are now with giving you too much information about the future."

"Perhaps not but let me think on that which you have already shared with me. Perhaps you can answer some other questions for me later?"

Closing his eyes for a while, he continued to ponder his situation with Rachael. He knew she was resting her blue gaze on his face. He wanted to believe in her. And he had no explanation why his suspicion of her had disappeared and he was now faced with liking what he saw. And trusting that she told the truth. He opened his eyes and found her gaze on him. She casually turned her head to look out the window of the carriage and he closed his eyes again. She was beautiful, magical, and captivating. Why? He wanted, no needed, to know more about her. This journey would be invaluable.

CROMDALE

The carriage came into the courtyard of the Castle Top Inn at Cromdale. It was a comfortable and quiet inn, where they could rest before going on to Aviemore. He watched to see if Rachael found it pleasing. He did not know why he wanted her approval but at the moment it mattered to him. The footman was down and opening the door of the carriage as it came to a stop. He came down the steps and turned to help his sister out. Putting his hand out to Rachael, he hoped she would take it despite her seeming reluctance. She did and he could feel the energy penetrate his hand and reach into his body. Oh yes. He was reacting to her in a very favourable way. He watched as a blush covered her face. He looked into her eyes and recognised that she too had felt the same reaction.

"Let me take you ladies indoors and I will arrange for our luncheon as you freshen up."

Both ladies turned and went through the door of the inn. The inn keeper, John Boag was waiting for them. The man had been his friend for as long as he could remember. His father and the previous inn keeper, Cameron Boag, John's father, had allowed the two boys to play together on the many trips that they had to Edinburgh. Now John was the innkeeper and he was laird. He greeted his friend.

"So good to see yee Laird Murray. I have a room for the ladies to freshen up." He called for his wife Fiona, and she took the ladies upstairs.

"It is good to see you John." He took his hand and shook it. Then he placed his hand on John's back.

"And you also, sir."

"Now John…"

"It just seems strange me calling you Duncan now that yee are the laird." John placed his hand on his back.

"I understand that John, but I'm still me, just Duncan. Remember?"

His friend laughed out loud and it was a joyous sound.

"Very well Duncan. Come into the back private room. It is a bit bigger for you and your ladies. Oh, and here is Alasdair come to join the party." John reached out to Alasdair and shook his hand.

"That's right, you old soak."

"It is good to see you too, my friend. Come in and join your brother, the laird." Then John laughed again as he headed down the hall to the back private room. The gentlemen followed.

"All is ready. When would you like your food to be brought out?" He stood to the side to allow the men to enter the room.

"Once the ladies have come down. And before you ask, one is my sister and the other is a visitor to the highlands."

"I know your sister. She has been here just as often with your father as you have. The other young lady is a very pretty little miss and I have no doubt that you have already noticed."

"Yes John. But enough." He smiled at his friend, making it clear that he had noticed but did not want to talk about it. He continued, "Can the horses be fed and watered? I think they can carry on to Aviemore this afternoon."

"I will get on to that immediately." He looked at Alasdair, "and your horse?"

"Already talked with your stable boy and he's being looked after as we speak."

"Is it your beautiful stallion, Black Robbie?" He asked Alasdair.

"My beautiful stallion." Duncan replied.

With that John left his guests laughing out loud.

Rachael looked around at the accommodation. She was delighted at how pretty, clean, and spacious their room was. She was glad to get her boots off. They were most definitely her size but a lot more confining than she was used to. She wished she could have worn her sneakers but that was out of the question. She was sitting on the chaise that was near the door as she took in the ambiance of the room. She was in a real travelling inn, and her excitement was beyond what she had expected. She placed her hand on the post of the bed. It was real. She was living in history It had beautiful dark wood and occupied the majority of the wall opposite. To her left was a window and to the right in the far corner a fireplace. She could feel the warmth from the small fire as it penetrated the room.

Glenna came and sat on the chaise next to her. She too took of her boots and breathed a sigh of relief as she put the boots on the ground.

"Oh, it feels good to have them off. I brought us light slippers to wear while we have our luncheon. We should take care of our ablutions as quickly as we can, so we don't keep my brothers waiting. Are you hungry?"

"Surprisingly, I am. We have done little but sit in the coach all morning, but I must say I am famished. Must be the sweet-smelling Scottish air." She gave a little laugh. Glenna giggled.

Rachael got up and went to the left corner of the room. There, she found fresh water to wash and a commode to relieve herself.

"They have everything we need."

"You do what you need to do to get ready. I will rest my head on the bed while you do so." Glenna went over to the bed and lay down with her back toward Rachael.

Rachael did as she was told finding the situation she was in distracting and extremely unusual. She could only imagine that for Glenna, travelling with another woman, this was standard and all too familiar.

They had been upstairs for nearly half an hour. She still had her watch that she kept in her reticule. It helped to ground her, remind her that she was not of this time. Though she sensed she was playing a part and it had become very familiar to her. They finally descended the stairs and were shown to the back room where they found Alasdair and Duncan waiting for them. The gentlemen each had an ale pot in front of them and seemed both relaxed and refreshed.

"Sorry to keep you waiting." She quietly greeted them with a curtsey. The gentlemen stood and bowed to them.

"Not at all. You have come down with plenty of time. John, can you bring in the luncheon?" Duncan directed his question to the innkeeper who stood in the doorway behind her.

Chairs were pulled out for her and Glenna and they went over to the table and sat down. She sat next to Duncan. She was getting used to his presence and his wanting to be near her. She wanted him to want to be near her and not just watch her.

Watching everyone relaxed, she was surprised they were not ready to get back on the road. "How long do you normally rest up?" She looked at Alasdair

It was Duncan who answered. "Some hours. We give the horses a real rest. But we have a team of four so they can go further this afternoon. So long as they eat and rest for a while. Why do you ask?"

"Nothing really. Just at home we would be on the road quickly so that many miles can be covered. Where I come from, we have many miles to travel." She really gave nothing away. She did not want to mention cars again. The two gentlemen looked at each other and she lowered her head. Glenna placed her hand on her thigh and gave it a little squeeze.

Before anything else could be said or done, a line of servants entered with trays of food. The plates were placed in the centre of the table. There were cold meats, cheeses, cream, and preserves. There were fruits both dried and fresh. Loaves of bread that filled the room with the freshly baked aromas. The spread looked wonderful. A glass of what she assumed was red wine was poured out for her and Glenna. The gentleman downed the last of their ales and glasses were poured for them also.

She could not believe all the wonderful food that lay on the table in front of her. She closed her eyes and took a deep breath and allowed all the mixed aromas to comfort her. She sighed.

"Oh, Mr Boag, you have out done yourself." She heard Glenna say.

"Is this to your satisfaction, miss?" She opened her eyes to see the inn keeper looking at her. He had asked her the question.

"I am sorry, sir. This is delightful. I am truly impressed. I had closed my eyes to concentrate on the wonderful aromas." He smiled, turned, and bowed to Duncan then Alasdair and then Glenna and herself and left the room.

"You have given him a great compliment," said Duncan. "It is simple fare."

"But this food is not simple. Homemade bread, preserves, and I bet he made his own cheese and cream."

"Yes, most people make their own." Duncan studied her face and added, "But not where you come from!"

"That's right." The heat rose to her face. "But let's not talk about that. Will you be happy to tell me all about the inn keeper? You and he seem to be good friends?" Duncan went on to explain their mutual childhood and the times they have spent together. How they both lost their fathers and had to take their fathers' place and both only in the last few years.

Rachael could begin to see that it was Duncan who had difficulty being the laird. It didn't sit right with him. He looked like he wanted to be somewhere else. Anywhere except in Buin Castle. She wanted to know more but realised she had to wait for him to tell her or a moment that was right when she could ask. She also noticed that the more he spoke of his life the more restless Alasdair became.

All too soon she and Glenna were again upstairs and preparing to continue their trip. More ablutions and boots placed back on their feet. They were soon sitting in the carriage waving to Mr Boag and his wife and were heading down the road to Aviemore.

***

Alasdair rode in the carriage again. He was telling stories and trying to get Rachael to join in the laughter. But she was finding that difficult. They were silly stories and nothing of a personal nature. His language and discussions were of a flirty nature. Not deep nor serious.

Occasionally Glenna would bring up things that they did as younger children. But Alasdair always changed the subject. There was no trust being shown to her by this man. He was not accepting her as Duncan had and she knew that was bothering Alasdair. She really didn't care. Alasdair made her feel uncomfortable.

The further she got from the Fairy Hill the more concerned she became that she might never get home. To her own time. Was she trapped here perhaps for the rest of her life? She just could not accept that, but she also knew that she was a stranger in this land, and she might never convince these people she was who she said she was. She had to stop thinking of them as friends. Well, not quite. She knew Glenna had a heart of gold and she believed in her. It was these gentlemen who didn't. But then Duncan...

She closed her eyes and wanted to drift off to sleep for a while. She must have. Because they were stopping to allow the horses to water. She was helped down by the footman and was again giving her legs a stretch. She walked away from the carriage to take in the views around her, but she soon noticed that she was not alone. Duncan was coming up from behind. She knew it was him by the way he walked. Solid, determined steps. She turned around and greeted him.

"You do not need to fear, Duncan, I'm not running away. Beside I could never run in these boots."

"I am aware that you are not trying to escape, Rachael. I wanted to talk with you privately if I may."

He looked at her and her heart melted. Why did he have this effect on her? Sure, he was tall and handsome and Scottish, just what she wished for up on Fairy Hill. The image of the man in the unfinished painting. But his personality made him so serious, so determined, even guarded. But she looked up into his green eyes and she melted inside. Every time she looked. When she was angry, sad, sick, or determined. It didn't matter. She would throw herself at him if she didn't say something and distract herself.

"What is it that you would like to talk to me about Duncan?" She waited patiently for him to begin.

"Firstly, I am sorry that the boots you are wearing are not as comfortable as the shoes we found you in on Fairy Hill. But they were so unusual that I was concerned that the servants might see them. They are well hidden in my room and I will give them back to you when we return to Castle Buin"

"Thank you. I had wondered where they had gotten too."

He began to pace back and forth in front of her. She waited for him to continue. He lifted his head a few times to look into her eyes. Oh, why did he look at her as if he wanted to hug her close?

"Can I suggest that we continue to walk?" They kept walking down the roadway on which they had already travelled in the coach. He continued to turn his head to stare at her. She really was going to melt if he continued to look at her that way. Were his eyes displaying longing, pleading? She wasn't sure what they displayed. Surely, she had to be imagining it? She closed her eyes and took a deep breath of the Scottish air that she loved so much. When she opened them again, he had stopped walking. She turned and he closed the gap between them and looked directly into her eyes.

"I wanted to tell you that I believe you."

"What, that I am from the future?"

"Yes. I know that others, Alasdair for one, will think me mad but I know from the clothing I found you in and the shoes you were wearing." He paused. "But also, the way you speak. The things you have said that are outrageous or knowledgeable, but not quite right."

"Thank you, I think?"

"That is what confuses me. You speak with a different vocabulary, which is not quite the way we speak. And your accent is like nothing I have ever heard before. Occasionally you slip into the way we speak but it feels as if you are play acting."

"Again, thank you, I think."

"What I am trying to say is that, despite my misgivings and confusion I will help you attempt to return to your own time when we return to my home. I believe you are from the future."

That got her attention.

"Really, I mean truly?" She lowered her head and closed her

eyes. This was not a dream. She clutched her hands in front of herself and opened her eyes and looked at him. He was telling the truth. This was no act. He believed her.

"Yes truly. I do not believe in fairies, I might add, but I do think that somehow you have come here from another time. It makes my head hurt just to think about it. It is not logical. But nothing else makes sense. You are from the future. So, if you will, I would like to hear more about your time. While we pay attention to the king, can you acquaint me with your world?"

This was the last thing she had expected, and she stared back into his eyes. A metaphorical bridge had been crossed. She threw her arms around his neck and planted a kiss on his adorable lips. Suddenly she let go and backed away from him. He stood there stiff as a pole.

"Oh Duncan, I am so sorry. I lost all thought. It is just that where I come from when someone tells you good news as you have just done, we often hug and kiss each other. Please forgive me. I did not mean to insult you or embarrass you." She watched as his face reddened but this was embarrassment not anger.

"Please calm yourself, Rachael. I admit I am a bit taken aback, but perhaps it would be interesting to learn more about this custom." He smiled with a hint of mischievousness. His shoulders relaxed and she grinned. This was better than she could have ever hoped for. He believed her.

He offered her his arm and they headed back to the carriage. She scanned the area and did not see anyone looking shocked or taken aback. Perhaps her actions had not been noticed. She again breathed a sigh of utter relief. Now, she wanted to find out why he didn't want to be laird. This man and the unfinished painting fascinated her. She would tell him of her world and hopefully she could find out what made him tick.

EDINBURGH

*S*unday 11*th* August 1822

Just as Duncan had said, the trip to Edinburgh took four days. But they were glorious days for her. Talking with freedom when Glenna and Duncan were together. But she kept her silence when Alasdair was nearby. Alasdair's personality still reminded her of her ex-boyfriend, so she was wary when he was around. Besides, he had declared to Glenna that he only pretended to believe her story. It was true that Duncan had made the same declaration but when he announced to her that he now believed, she sensed the truth in that declaration. But being able to speak freely with the others had made her content and happy.

The last part of the trip into Edinburgh was the most different for her. No bridge scanned the Firth of Forth. It was strange to cross the water in a ferry. She knew that there had been one, but it was still not what she imagined. The city seemed duller and dirtier than the modern city of her time. It still spread itself out over the plains and hills that surrounded Arthurs Seat. But the buildings were of poor quality and poverty seemed to be all around her.

So, when on the end of the fourth day they pulled up in front of the Edinburgh house of the Murray's Aunt, she had not expected to see a place that she knew. It was in the new part of the city, known as New Town. This was recognisable to her. The streets were similar but less chaotic to the Edinburgh she knew. No cars or buses but plenty of horse drawn carriages and carts. People wandered around everywhere. When they entered Charlotte Square, she became animated.

"In my time," she said, glad that Glenna and Duncan were in the carriage, "there is a house that is made to look like what a town house looks like now. Do you understand? I will actually see how well the National Trust have done their research."

Duncan looked confused at her words but soon was smiling with her as the excitement penetrated the carriage. The carriage pulled up in front of No.7.

"You are joking. You own No.7? Well your aunt does. Oh boy, I can't wait to see how the house looks."

"What do you mean? How it looks?"

"Duncan and Glenna, I am so excited. Your home becomes a museum in my time. A museum that shows us how you live now. I visited this house when I was in Edinburgh last week. Well, it was last week in my time." She gave her head a little shake. "This is truly unbelievable. The city is so big, but you actually live where I have been in my future."

"Tell me, has it changed? I mean, when you walk through the house with me later today, can you tell me what the rooms look like in your time. I would like to know what your time thinks or believes of the way we live. This is my aunt's house, but we use it when she is in the highlands. She is there at the moment, as she has no intention of seeing the king." They slowly came out of the carriage, stretching and straightening their clothing.

"Does she dislike the king so much?" Rachael asked while watching to see the reaction Duncan would give to her question. Duncan looked at her and smiled.

"Very few English are liked by the Scots. We have our reasons." Duncan offered his arm to Rachael and they ascended the stairs.

The butler stood at the front door waiting to welcome the master of the Murray clan into his aunt's Edinburgh home.

"Welcome Laird Murray. Tea awaits you in the day room."

She leaned over and whispered. "On the first floor."

He smiled down at her. "Yes, my dear, as it is in most houses in Charlotte Square and nearly every distinguished house in town."

"Thank you, MacArthur. If you will escort the ladies to their rooms so they can freshen up."

He turned to them and bowed. "Please join us in the day room when you have refreshed."

She followed MacArthur to the second floor and what would be her bed chamber while she was here. Her room was next to Glenna for which she was grateful. Within fifteen minutes she was ready to go down to the day room. She went to Glenna's door and knocked on it.

Glenna opened it. "Good, you are ready. So am I."

Their rooms were at the back of the house and Glenna pointed to her brothers' rooms at the front of the house as they made their way to the stairwell. Then before they descended, she opened another door to the left of the stairs.

"And in this room is the water closet. We have all the modern conveniences here in Edinburgh."

Rachael looked in and what she saw astounded her. It looked very much like an elaborate toilet. Glenna mistook her quietness as confusion for her not wanting to use it.

"You may continue to use the chamber pot if you like."

"Oh no. I'm happy to use a toilet, I mean the water closet."

They smiled and then they laughed out loud and headed down to the dayroom.

The dayroom was bright and airy and from what she could remember from the house when she had visited it in the future. It was like what she remembered, though not exactly the same. Colours were different, still pastel in nature, but she was unsure that the colours were the same as the future. But there was also more furniture and knick knacks. Things that personalised the rooms. More things to distinguish people's likes and personalities. Except in the future they called it a parlour if she remembered correctly, as they did in Victorian times. Her head was starting to hurt again.

She let out a deep sigh to be finally sitting down and having a cup of tea. She didn't miss not having coffee anymore. She enjoyed the tea from this period and knew how valuable it was to all who served it and drank it. It was a pleasure she knew that not a lot of other people had in this period. It was more common than it had been fifty years earlier but still a special pleasure that she delighted in.

Conversation was stilted again due to Alasdair being with them. He continued to try to engage her in conversation to draw her out. But she feigned tiredness. But they relaxed after a time as the early evening light shifted in the sky. Glenna and Alasdair soon departed to their rooms to rest and she found herself alone with a man she had grown extremely fond of in the past days. A man who had said he believed in her and he wanted to know more from where she had come from. She smiled as he got straight into conversation with her.

"Can you tell me the country where you came from?" Duncan settled back in his chair to await her response.

She took a deep breath. "You have heard of Australia. Well, that is where I come from."

He sat upright. "You are a convict then." He looked shocked.

"No." She added quickly. "In the future we are a land of free people. My family immigrated to Australia in the 1950's. It is a big nation and still good friends with England. The queen is still our Queen." She chose her words carefully, trying to think about how he would hear what she was saying.

"So, you have a Queen on the throne. I hope she is better than the fat king who spends all our money now." He looked at her and she could sense his hatred for the king.

"She is much loved and is the longest serving monarch in English history." She smiled at his surprised look and then continued.

"I live in a city called Dubbo in central New South Wales. I work as a lawyer and also write books."

"A woman lawyer! That is what you meant when you said client the other evening. I have not known that women could... But in your time."

"Yes. Women in my time can be whatever we want to be. There are many things that exist in my time that you will know nothing of. Employment. People do not have such wealth that they do not need to work. Well, very few have. But lots of land holdings are not as big as they are now."

He was pensive, perhaps thinking on what she had revealed. She waited for a moment before she continued, allowing what she had said to sink in.

"I'm not sure that it will help you understand if you are unsure what I am discussing with you. Do you wish for me to continue?"

"Do not fret. I am sure that you speak the truth. So, describe the countryside where you live." He paused, looking into her eyes, and continued, "Please."

She looked at him as he smiled. She did want him to know how she had lived. She wanted him to know almost everything about her.

"Well, that is easier to do. It is farmland. But not as you know. We grow wheat and canola and raise sheep. There is mining in the area too. But the city I live in is big and services a large area around it. It is very dry and hot in the summer. Our grass is less green and the climate much drier." She hesitated. "I mean we don't have the kind of rainfall that is common here in Scotland. In fact, we have had very severe droughts in the last 20 years. And we do not have such lush pastures. But the skies look really big and are more often than not, beautiful and blue." She suddenly had pangs of homesickness. She wanted to take him at that moment to her home and show him what she was describing. "I wish I could take you home and show you what the future is like, even down to the water closet." He laughed with her. "Truly I would love to show you."

"That would be delightful. Or perhaps I am unable to travel to the future. Perhaps there is a reason you have come through time. A quest and not just an adventure. Perhaps the Fairy Hill works only for you."

She leaned back into her chair to ponder his comment. "You surprise me. I did not think that you were capable of believing that a woman could perform any quest."

He stood and began to walk around the room. She could see that he was thinking deeply as she looked at him.

He stopped to gaze down at her. "I know that men are usually the ones who have great adventures and quests, but I know that my mother came to Scotland on a great adventure and her quest was to raise our little family. For her it was a great adventure. Do you understand what I mean?"

"I do." She closed her eyes to try to imagine what his mother looked like. And as if he read her mind, he continued. She opened her eyes.

"The portrait above the fireplace is my mother and father. I miss them both. My mother died when I was twelve years old and my father but two years ago. She was such a beautiful woman." He wandered over to stand in front of the portrait. "Not just her physical beauty but she was a woman that many admired. Because she had a generous spirit and a heart full of love for us and so many others."

Rachael got up and stood next to him so that she too could study the painting. His mother was beautiful. Her dark black hair reflected the light that was all around her. Her colouring was so like Duncan and Alasdair. His father, so tall and proud again showing her the influence that he had on his sons. He was a man who was distinguished as well as wealthy. But his colouring was Glenna to a tee. Glenna had his tall statue and most definitely his colouring. The light auburn of his hair reflected Glenna. They were dressed in their finest clothing, high fashion of their time. And they were young. She guessed that it had been painted just before or after they married. But most definitely before children.

Duncan placed his hand lightly on her shoulder. "My parents had a deep love for each other. Father had this portrait done just after they were married. My aunt wishes to keep it here until her death. It is her sister after all. Then it will return to the castle. It is one of my favourites. The other painting that is my favourite, is of all of us when Glenna was but a bairn. It was painted just before our mother died. It is back at the castle in my bedroom."

She looked up and studied his face as he gazed at the painting before him, no doubt thinking of the one that was back in his bedroom. He turned his head and looked at her. She wanted to know of the unfinished painting. It was then that she noticed the covered easel in the very corner of the room.

"May I ask if that unfinished painting is of you?"

"It is of me. And it is yet to be completed. Why do you ask?"

"Well, if I am correct then I know the painting. I saw it some years ago in an antique shop here in Edinburgh. And if I can tell you the colours of what you were wearing then you know that I speak the truth in case you still doubt me."

"I do not doubt you. But please tell me." He walked toward the painting.

The words came rushing from her as if she had to get them out before she burst into flames.

"Your hair is curling on to your necktie. You do not have a day coat on which I know is very unusual. But a glorious golden yellow evening coat. It is extremely flamboyant." she closed her eyes as if summoning up the image before her. "It is an embossed material. So wonderful…"

He took the cover off the painting and there was her painting. The painting that she had fallen in love with years ago. He came and stood in front of her. And now she was in front of the man that was the painting. Did she dare tell him that she had loved him almost all her life? His luscious green eyes gazing into her own.

"You are correct. The coat is yellow and formal to match our kilt. We have a blue, green kilt with lines of yellow flowing through it." He took her into his arms. "Can you tell me why I am attracted to you? As if I have known you all my life? Why thinking of your beautiful face makes me want to run through the hills declaring my love for you?"

The heat rose to her face. He had said what she had so longed to hear.

"Duncan?" She had not expected such a declaration. Her stomach was doing summersaults as she continued to gaze into his eyes. Not a painting but the real man whom she had gotten to know on their trip here.

"I apologise for my forward speech, but I feel we have little time. In fact, time seems to be very important to me at the moment. I know it is to you." His hands rested gently around her waist. But heat flowed from him into every part of her body. She studied his eyes and could see the longing. Did she dare have an affair with a man in another time? Isn't it what she wanted more than anything? She gave into the longing within her chest.

She put her arms around his waist. He looked down into her face and she could see the desire in his eyes. His arms went around her, and he held her closer than she had ever been held before. He slowly pulled away from her and his lips descended to hers. The heating of her blood now reached into every part of her being, filling every part of her as he deepened the kiss. It was gentle and timid to begin with. But soon his tongue began to explore her lips and mouth and it became a deeper exploration. Her soul rose to his lips and caressed every part of his mouth with a desire that she had never known. This man had captured her very being with one kiss and her body was begging for more. But all too quickly the kiss was over. She was bereft, totally alone, though he still held her in his arms.

"I have never felt the longing for any woman the way I feel about you at this moment. I want you…no I need you. All of you."

She held him close to her and whispered, "I too have never felt like this before. Do we dare to be together? Will time be willing to let us have such a wonderful experience?"

"Do you wish to make love with me, Rachael?"

"More than anything." He looked deeper into her eyes than anyone else had managed. She had no doubt that he saw the truth of her declaration. No doubt.

"I will come for you tonight and bring you to my bed. I want to feel every part of you." He leaned down again and kissed her gently on the lips. Barely touching and creating more desire to have him than she had known of any man. Her tongue caressed his bottom lip. He drew his head away, staring at her, but held her close to his body. His erection was warm and hard on her belly and she leaned ever closer into his embrace. He slowly parted them.

"I will come when we all are in bed. Wait for me." He was suddenly serious and his usual self. He bowed and left the room.

She was standing on a precipice. If she took one step forward, she would fall. She clutched a nearby chair and lowered herself into it. She tried to gain control of her rapidly beating heart. She had nothing more on her mind than to be in bed with Duncan. Was that why she was here, to know what true love could be like? Could she stay with him forever rather than return to the future? There were too many questions and her desire refused to allow her to think straight. She had a lot to ask those darn fairies.

She went to the table, picked up her teacup and drained the last of its contents. She filled it again with tea that was stronger than she usually drank and downed the contents. One of the servants came into the room and asked if he could clear the table. She barely heard him but nodded. She rose and left the room and went upstairs to dress for supper. Assuming she didn't self-combust on the way.

ONE TRUE LOVE

What had he done? Oh, he wanted her more than any woman he had ever known. But he had invited her to his bed in his aunt's family home. Could he keep her as his own? Was she really from the future? Too many questions. His blood was boiling and driving him to the privacy of his aunt's small study.

He wanted to feel every inch of that beautiful body she possessed. He closed the door and leaned against the back of it. The sun was going down and the golden pink shades of the evening penetrated the room. They only reminded him of her and his wanting. He went to the sideboard and poured himself a large whisky.

He sat behind the desk but the lust that filled his being would not abate. He will have her regardless of the consequences. He loved her. Why? He did not know but he did. He remembered the words of his father.

"When you find the woman that you cannot live without, it will hit you as if a bolt from the sky. Then you will know the joy I had with your mother. I want for you to have that kind of love."

He had never believed those words. Could not imagine for a moment what his father had felt. Until now. Rachael was everything he wanted. Beautiful, kind, intelligent and above all captivating. From the moment he had seen her, despite his anger and confusion he had wanted her. He could not explain how she had captivated him. Why had she had come to him?

He knew why he wanted his brother to stay away from her and not attempt to make her another of his conquests. He wanted that pleasure. He wanted her more than life itself. He wanted no one else near her. The need to hold her in his arms forever was greater than any emotion he had ever had. Even his earlier anger toward her. But her story. The things she said and believed as truth. He wanted to believe it. He needed to believe it. He had told her he had but now was unsure. She was still the same selfless lady, the same woman who had said she would only tell him the truth. But the doubt that she had told nothing, but truth penetrated his thoughts. He wanted to believe, he truly did. He must if they would be together. He went and sat behind the desk.

There was a knock at the door and Alasdair entered. "Can I intrude, brother?"

"Yes. What is it that you want?" He spoke the words more harshly than he intended. "I'm sorry, Alasdair. My mind is elsewhere. What is it that you would speak to me about?"

"Are you well? You seem somewhat flushed." He came and sat in the chair opposite to his.

Duncan was glad he was sitting behind the desk so that his brother could not detect his arousal. How would he explain that?

"I am fine, just distracted."

"Is it the Miss Rachael who distracts you?"

His brother could always see through his head and read his thoughts. If there was such a thing as fairies, he would swear his brother had their blood in his veins. The ability to know what a person was thinking. He sighed.

"Yes. She has been able to do that to me since she arrived. But forget my thoughts. What of your own?"

"I took the liberty of instructing cook to provide us with a light supper as our luncheon was rather a royal feast. I then wish to see some of my friends this evening. As we will be involved in the king's functions over the coming weeks, I would like to catch up with them in a more relaxed circumstance."

He knew exactly what kind of relaxed circumstances his brother was envisaging. The same thoughts and position he wished to be in with Rachael. But this suited his purposes. One less person in the house to complicate his plans for the evening. He only needed to distract Glenna.

"That is fine, Alasdair. I plan for an early evening so that I can deal with the great pile of mail that has arrived." He pointed to the bundle of letters and cards on the desk. "They can wait till tomorrow, but I will need to accept or apologise for certain events in the morning. We can meet at luncheon tomorrow to discuss the upcoming plans. If that is suitable?"

"Thank you, Duncan. That sounds amicable. I will let the ladies know that we eat in an hour." With that Alasdair left his study. He wondered, and not for the first time, why he allowed his brother to do some of the organising for the farms, the house, and the family. Glenna had played her part but almost without knowing Alasdair had slipped into some of those roles. The fire in his being that had been raging when his brother had entered, had dropped to a smoulder but he knew that at a moment's notice or at the sight of Rachael it would flare again. He heard a voice in the passage outside the door and Glenna's head appeared around it.

"Duncan, I understand we will have supper shortly. If you are agreeable, I wish to have an early night. I want to go and do some last-minute shopping for Rachael in the morning." She came into the room.

"That will be agreeable. Rachael could probably do with an early night herself. And as for the shopping, be sure that you get several evening dresses for her. And charge them to me. I want her to have the best." He stood as Glenna came over and hugged him.

"That is so generous of you. Thank you." She looked up into his eyes. "Are you aware of her feelings for you?"

"I am not sure what you mean." He knew what she was hinting at but had no desire or intention to discuss it with his sister.

"I believe that she has fallen in love with you, brother." She turned and headed for the door. She looked back at him. "Treat her carefully. She is more to you than you can imagine."

That made no sense to him. How could she be more than what he already believed her to be? The love of his life who he might lose if what she says is true and that she is from the future. He continued to ponder his sister's words. He shook his head, finished his drink, and then went to change for supper

---

"It will be wonderful to see all my friends. And I assume that I will not be home till early morning. I may stay out all night."

"So, you will be partying." She paused, shook her head. "Forget that. I hope you have a wonderful time." Rachael smiled but Alasdair did not return the pleasure.

Alasdair gave her a sour look. They were all tired from the travel, but good manners still needed to be applied.

He was fooling himself. He was worried that Alasdair's dislike of her would make their being together difficult. She seemed distracted and he was glad that his brother would not be in the house this evening.

Glenna stood. "I'm for bed. Sleep as long as you wish, Rachael. We will have a late breakfast and then we can go do some shopping." Glenna smiled at Rachael.

"Thanks, Glenna. That will be delightful. Sleep well."

Glenna left the room. Alasdair stood, bowed, and headed towards the door. Then he turned to them.

"Have a relaxing evening. I plan to party, is that right?" He looked at Rachael and grinned his rakish grin.

"That's right. Have a wonderful evening."

Finally, they were alone. He had waited for what seemed like days to finally be able to talk to her. It had been but a few hours since he had kissed her. He waited for the servants to clear the table and then asked them to bring in the tea. He stood and knelt at her feet.

"My darling Rachael. Are you certain that you wish to be with me tonight?"

She looked at him and placed her hand on his shoulder. "Of course. You are the reason I'm here, I believe. I know what I wished for when I fell asleep on the hill and you are my answer to that wish. Your painting was what I had on my mind. It brought me to you. But you? Is this what you want? I do not want you to feel any obligation to me."

"How can I not? It is true that I had been to the hill many times, asking why my life had changed. Why I could not continue to study. I knew that one day I would be laird, but it came much sooner than I expected. I had no one who could share the burden with me and no sign of any woman in my future. Father's accident was so unexpected and so devastating for me." He got up and sat in the seat next to her. All his concentration was on her.

"Believe me Duncan, I do understand. I have many friends but no family. My parents died not very long ago, and I miss them deeply. No one to share my successes with, to talk to and to ask their advice. You at least have your sister and brother. I have no other family. I am an only child." He stood and reached his hand down to hers. He drew her into his arms holding her closer than he had held anyone.

"That is true, but I could never tell them that I do not want to be laird." He looked down into her eyes. "I have always done what is expected of me, but I honestly do not desire to be like my father. I do not believe I ever can be. It is if I was meant for something else. I just don't know what." He pulled her back into his embrace and continued to hold her close. "I have never told anyone my desire not to be laird. I ask that you do not tell my brother or sister of my thoughts."

"You know that your secret is safe with me. Perhaps I am here to help you find the answer to what you seek."

He hoped so.

They went to the other side of the room to the chaise, while the servants cleaned away the remaining supper dishes. A pot of tea and two cups was placed on a small table in front of them. They did not speak while the servants completed the assigned tasks. Soon they were alone again.

"I have never known anyone like you. You are a strong woman who knows her own mind. That does not scare me as it would other men that I know. My mother was strong. But kind-hearted and beautiful as you are. Some men want a woman to just do what they are told and keep their mouths closed. Not I. You are intelligent and beautiful, and I want to know all your thoughts." She poured the tea for them both.

He took a moment to let the words that he had revealed penetrate her consciousness. She looked longingly at him and he knew that this beautiful woman was for him. She handed him his cup.

"Duncan, I barely know you. And you seem to know me better than I do myself. If I am the person you describe then...wow I must be kind of special."

"You are special and yes the way I describe you is what I see."

"As for my knowing you, I feel I have known you all my life. Though I didn't expect you to be as angry as when we first met. But please know I want you more than you realise." She took a sip from her cup. "Please try to understand what I mean." She hesitated. He waited patiently for her next words. "You are not like any of the men in my time. You respect me for who I am, even if you don't fully understand it. But can I ask you to wait before we discuss any more? I wish to bathe and then wait for you to come and get me. I want to be in your arms and your bed before we say anymore. I want you to not only know what I say is true but to feel it."

He leaned over and kissed her gently. They put their cups on the table.

"Very well, my Rachael. Your wish is my command." He stood up and went to the bell pull. A footman came in and he issued instructions for her bath to be prepared. She stood and curtsied.

"Until later." He bowed and she left the room.

The house was still. It was some hours since he had seen her, but he had waited patiently so that nothing would intrude on their time together. The servants were in their rooms below stairs and Glenna had been in bed for some time. Alasdair would not return till late in the morning, jolly and content.

He left his room and walked quietly and slowly to Rachael's bedroom door. He could see a light coming from under the closed door. He did not knock but quietly opened it and stepped inside. She stood as he entered and came over to him. She slipped her arms around his waist. He had no coat on and was dishevelled in comparison to his usual state. But she seemed happy to see him.

"I wasn't sure that you would come. I know that women are not to be so forward in this time but believe me I wanted you here." She hugged him again.

"I said that I would come. Now blow out your candle and we will go to my bed. I want that more than anything else."

She did. The house had gas light installed two years previous, yet she had told him that she preferred the candlelight. It was more romantic she had said. They still used candlelight at the castle but things in Edinburgh were far more modern. She, however preferred the candlelight. He adored that. He could not wait for her to see his room and the many candles that lit it. Quietly, he opened the door and holding her hand drew her out into the corridor. They slowly made their way to his room and entered. Only one floorboard creaked. Both of them had stood stock still but nothing had happened, so they continued. Once inside his room he locked the door to prevent the arrival of any servants or his drunken brother.

He turned around and took her into his arms. Then placing his hand under her chin, he lifted her head and repeated the exploration of her mouth and lips that he had begun that afternoon. Neither moved but just held each other tightly while he explored the kiss that he had longed to repeat. After a time, he stopped and whispered into her ear.

"I have longed for this day. To find my true love and I have no doubt that it is you. I know that we have but just met, but I am certain in my heart." He reached down and caressed her neck with kisses and began to taste her. She moaned quietly and pushed herself further into his body. He too, moaned. He reached down and began to lift the cotton night gown that she had on. He touched her bottom and found nothing in his way. He began to knead her lusciousness.

Never had he wanted anyone so much. He had had other women but for his own benefit and relief. They had meant little to him. But now that he had Rachael in his arms all he wanted was to make her moan till she could scream her release. Her pleasure was what would give him the pleasure he had longed for. That is what he wanted and desired.

"Come, let me see your beauty." He took her hand and drew her to the bed. He undid the buttons at the top of her night dress and lifted it up over her head. The candlelight made her body glow and appear as gold.

What beauty.

"You have so many candles lit. Why?" she asked, her voice husky from the kiss.

"It is romantic, so I have been told, and I must agree with you, it is. But I also want to see the beauty of your body. I have longed since your arrival to see you thus." He could see her blush but loved her bashfulness.

"I have dreamed that one day I would find a man that I could love, who would love me for who I am and not what I can do. Thank you, Duncan."

He took off his shirt and removed his trousers and then he too stood before her with no clothing to hinder her view. Her gaze caressed each part of his body and she seemed well pleased. He drew her to his manhood and pressed her against it. Then quickly he lifted her up and placed her on the bed. Exploring the rest of her body was his next desire. And that would take a lifetime.

The house was quiet and still. He held Rachael in his arms as she slept. This was a woman who had experienced a man before. That disturbed him. He would ask her about her previous lovers. He knew that he had experienced other women and that she too had the right to choose her own partners. But to know that he was not the first troubled his sensibilities.

Rachael stirred. She looked around, smiling at him, and sat up. Her blonde hair hung around her shoulders and caressed her breasts, that were naked before him. He reached out and cupped a breast in his hand.

"What troubles you, Duncan?" Her quiet question did not

surprise him. She had a way of seeing into his heart. Those blue eye would forever penetrate his soul.

"I am not your first." She smiled at him, but it was a smile of concern, not triumph.

"No, you are not but you are the first that I love. I said that I would be truthful with you. And I will. In the future, people share love making more often with many partners. I didn't. I had one partner, but he did not love me. I thought he did, but I was wrong. He wanted to own me. I wish I had waited for you, but I didn't."

"Did you love him?"

She lowered her head and he could see that she was thinking how to answer that question. He gave her as much time as she needed. He knew she would say the truth. She had promised. And he wanted to believe that more than anything else in his life.

"I will admit to you that I thought I did at the time. But I didn't. It was the excitement of having someone say they loved me, I think." She leaned over and kissed his forehead. "But I am not your first either. You have knowledge and techniques to pleasure me that you didn't get from a book." Her smile penetrated his soul. "You seem well practiced. Is it acceptable for you to lay with a woman but I can't lay with a man?"

"I was contemplating that when you woke. No, it is not fair. It is just the way our world is. It is the tradition of marriage and love. Men explore and women wait to be found. But I do have one desire, I want to be your last. I do not want you to have any other man but me. Which means that you will be staying with me or I will be going with you, to the future."

Her smile reached her lips but not her eyes.

"That is a big decision." She declared. "I want you to be sure it is love that is talking. Be sure it is me you want to be with. Please think hard before you decide."

He looked deep into her eyes and was sure she was his one. He wanted her by his side for whatever his future held. Would the fairy folk allow him to go to the future? Was he now admitting that there were such folk? He had denied it for so long. He looked into her pools of blue.

"I have never ever felt like this about any other woman. I want to hold on to you forever. Please stay with me, or allow me to come with you?"

Rachael laid down and reached her arms around the man she loved more than anything in the world. Could she stay? Could she give up her life in the future to be with him in the past? Those questions went quickly through her mind. Look at what he had done. So many candles in the room because she had said it was romantic. He had roses filling the vases and the fragrance penetrated the whole room to its corners. This was his room and he had made it hers for the night. He had wanted this time with her just as much as she had.

"Yes Duncan. I will stay." She whispered.

"Then will you marry me as soon as can be arranged?"

"But Duncan, we know so little about each other. Don't you want time to be sure?"

"I beg to differ, my dear. I know there is no other woman in the world I could love more than you. Marry me. Let me show you how much I love you. Let me show you for the rest of our lives." He pulled her into his arms.

IS IT LOVE?

M*onday 12th August 1822*

Rachael had quietly escaped to her room as Duncan slept. This was all so quick. Did he really love her enough perhaps for him to return with her? Or would she stay here with him? She had said she would. Her head was hurting again. She slipped into her bed but could not sleep. Dawn had already come, and she could hear the quiet movement of the servants' downstairs. She was not sure what time it was but hoped she could still get some sleep. Sometime later, she finally heard someone in the passage.

A maid slipped into her room and opened the curtains. Light filled her room and she stretched in her bed pretending she had just woken. Perhaps she just had. Another maid came in with a cup of tea. She enjoyed her morning 'cuppa' and had asked if it could be brought to her. Being the guest to a laird had its advantages and she was sure that she would see more of that displayed in the coming days. If she should accept his proposal.

She was comfortably sore in all the right places. She slipped out of bed and went to the wash basin to freshen up. She looked in the mirror and was surprised to see the glow radiating from her. Was it so obvious that she had been well loved last night? She looked around to see if any of the servants had noticed. No one paid her any attention. She washed and dressed in the yellow gingham dress that no longer fitted Glenna. She sat at the dressing table and the maid helped her fix her hair. Now and then the maid would glance at her and blush. She hoped that the girl was nervous and not thinking about what Rachael had been up to during the night. She looked in the mirror again and watched her own colour rise from her neck to her face. She picked up her cup and drank from it. Then she closed her eyes.

She opened them again when the door opened, and a fully dressed Glenna came in. Rachael briefly looked at her friend.

"Did you sleep well?" Glenna asked with a big knowing smile across her face. Rachael closed her eyes again.

"Well enough," Rachael answered, keeping her eyes tightly closed. She did not want to reveal what she had really been doing through the night.

"And my brother, did he sleep well?" She no doubt was grinning like a Cheshire cat, but Rachael did not want to open her eyes to find out. She took some deep breaths and still could smell the roses from the other room. Nothing was going to let her forget what she did last night.

"That you will need to ask your brother. How would I know?"

She peeked at her friend then looked quickly at the maid and watched the maid go bright red. In a few moments, the maid finished her hair, curtseyed, and left the room.

Nothing more was said until the maid had closed the door.

"I know that you were with my brother last night and I could not be more delighted. He needs you. You are just the kind of woman that he will love forever."

Rachael sat there shocked at what she had heard Glenna say. How could she know? They had been so careful.

"I woke during the night and saw you with my brother going into his room. If he has taken you to his bed, then he is most seriously in love with you. He would have stayed in your room if he did not respect and care for you. Don't you see? He wants you for wife."

Rachael sat looking at Glenna's reflection in the mirror. The girl was young and far too romantic for her own good.

"You need to be very careful what you say, Glenna. If what you say is true, I do not believe that Duncan will be happy if you voice that opinion. He was trying to be discreet." Rachael hung her head and hoped that the red of her face was diminishing.

"That is why I am here and not in his bedroom asking my questions. It is obvious that you two love each other. It has become obvious to all of us over the last four days of travelling together. We have watched your love grow."

Rachael put her face in her hands. Surely not everyone will notice. She did not want all commenting and perhaps embarrassing Duncan.

"Do not fret future sister. Oh, I like that. Future sister, in more ways than one, is it not? Let us go to breakfast. We have a busy day ahead of us."

Rachael gave up. She looked in the mirror again just to be sure that she did not have 'I had sex with the laird' written all over her face.

The two ladies made their way down to the breakfast room. Alasdair was sitting at the table as was Duncan. Rachael was sure she went bright red as she came into the room. She could feel that damn heat rising from her neck.

"Good morning, dear ladies," Alasdair chortled. "I do hope you slept better than I. I have been up all night and had a very jolly time with my friends."

Rachael could agree he had a joyous time. His hair had not been brushed and he looked as though he had been in his clothes all night. He was a sight. Duncan however was his usual clean shaven, dressed in clean clothes and ready for the business of the day. Just as he always was. No indication of something unique and marvellous happening to him during the evening.

"So long as you had a grand time, Dair dear." Glenna was smiling and giggling as she sat in the seat next to him.

Rachael sat in the seat that Duncan had stood and pulled out for her. She looked into his eyes and smiled at him as she sat down. He returned that longing smile. A knowing smile just for her and she sighed deeply that his loving look was still there. Duncan remained standing.

"I am glad that we are all together. We are but days away from the king arriving and we have much to do. Firstly, I want you to know of my intention to marry Rachael as soon as we are able."

Rachael watched as Alasdair's joy turned to disbelief and Glenna began clapping. Her stomach sank and she wished she had stayed upstairs. She had no idea that Duncan was going to announce their affection for each other straight away. She was annoyed that he hadn't said. And she was still thinking things through. Had she said yes? She thought for a moment. She had.

"Tell me I did not hear what you just said, brother? You are to marry a stranger whom we do not kin?"

"None of us *kin* strangers' brother, but Rachael is known to me. I love her and wish to marry as soon as we can."

Alasdair stood. He shook his head, first slowly and then with more speed. "You are crazy, man. We know not where she comes from. Perhaps she means to steal the estate of the Murrays. Or she is a spy for the king? Only days ago, you thought that. You cannot be seriously considering such an outrageous plan."

Duncan remained standing, placing his hands behind his back. He had an air of confidence that Rachael wished she had at this moment. "I love Rachael and intend to marry her. You had best get used to the idea."

"I will not." Alasdair now stood and matched his brother's stance.

"Can I say something please," Rachael pleaded. Alasdair turned on her.

"You have bewitched my brother. I will nay listen to ye." His Scottish accent was coming to the fore. "I will no have you turn this family upside down." His face was redder than she imagined her own to be. She could not understand the fierce anger that poured from him. She could understand the distress from the speed of the announcement but not the anger. Why was he so angry? If Duncan was in love, then surely as laird it was his decision.

"Let her speak and I suggest you listen, Dair." Glenna stood and came to stand next to Rachael's chair. Rachael again felt the pressure of those who stood around her. But she did love Duncan and wanted to be with him. She was driven. Driven into a dream she could not wake up from. She took in some deep breaths and spoke softly.

"Alasdair, please know that I have no intention of turning this family upside down. I have grown so fond of you all. Well Duncan, I have fallen in love with him. There is no man on earth both in this time and my own that I love as I love Duncan." She was proud of herself that she could voice the truth despite her misgivings.

"Oh, we are to hear about this future nonsense again. Duncan, the woman is mad. What would mother or father say about this nonsense? You know nothing about her. It has been but days!" He was pacing back and forth. He looked like a caged beast ready to strike at anyone who got too close. She did not want to be his target.

She looked at Duncan who was holding his temper at bay. She took him by the hand and watched him calm himself. Could she help him to control his temper? That was unexpected. Perhaps she was sent here to be just that. A catalyst for him to control his emotions. Would that help him to be a better laird?

"I believe that father would adore her and welcome her into the family. And mother also."

"I will not. You will regret this." He looked directly at her and she felt the cold that penetrated from his gaze. He hated her. That was it. He hated her. "The Murray clan will not have this." He threw down his napkin on the table and stormed from the room.

Duncan squeezed her hand. "Sorry, my love."

"I will go talk to him." Glenna said as she headed toward the door.

"No Glenna. Let him cool down first. He needs to come to terms with my announcement. Once he has slept, he will see things more clearly. Besides, I need you to help me this morning."

Glenna came and sat down back into the chair she had been in before. The servants entered and served the young women their breakfast. She had another cup of tea placed in front of her. She picked up the cup and lets its warmth take the chill from her hands. That chill settled throughout her bones. This was not a great way to start. Strife could follow them if this were not cleared up and soon. The servants left and the conversation continued.

"Duncan please, this is all so hurried. May I please make a suggestion?"

He was now seated in the chair next to her. She put the cup back on the table and he took her hands in his.

"Of course, so long as you still wish to marry me?"

"I do, but the king's visit will be taking up much of everyone's time. So, introduce me as your fiancé, but let us wait with the marriage till we return to Castle Buin, please? We must give Alasdair time to adjust."

She hoped her pleadings would show him that she was determined not to rush the marriage. She loved him and knew he loved her too. She looked into his eyes. "I am determined that we do it this way." She said the words with little conviction. She was concerned that a rift had occurred and that she was the cause.

"If that is what you wish, then that is what we will do." He lifted her hand and kissed her fingers gently. "But be assured, I will not let you change your mind." It seemed he could be encouraged to think of others when he was determined to have his own way. That boded well.

None of that discussion had gone the way he had intended but he was determined to make Rachael his own and convince his brother that he knew Rachael, the real Rachael.

"I for one am delighted. The fae have brought you your love and I couldn't be happier." Duncan smiled at his sister. He could not be angry at her about the fae. Besides, he was starting to believe that she could be right. Rachael was a gift. A gift that the fae may very well have given him.

"I believe you may be right, Glenna. Now will you arrange the carriage? We are going shopping."

THERE IS ALWAYS SHOPPING

The day had passed as a blur. Duncan and Glenna escorted her around town to milliners and dress makers for evening and day wear. Every item that a lady of class and distinction could want, Duncan made sure that she had. Edinburgh was a boisterous and busy place. Much as it would be in two hundred years' time. He introduced her to friends and other landed gentry they met on their travels around the town. She was from a family of distinction in the Australian colonies he told them. Everyone was friendly and delighted to make her acquaintance. They asked her many questions of the colony and she did her best to give them the correct impression.

She was delighted that they had lunch at White Hart Inn and by the time they reached home they were all very much exhausted. She was and could see the same on both Glenna and Duncan. As they came up the steps of No 7., she saw Alasdair waited for them.

"Oh, Dair we have had such a glorious day. It is such a pity that you could not join us. It has been such fun."

Glenna was excited and Rachael was sure she did not notice the icy glare he levelled at them all.

"Duncan, I wish to speak with you."

Duncan paused as he ascended the top step. "What about Dair?"

"That, sir, is private. Between you and I." Alasdair placed his hands behind his back and stood as tall as he could, waiting for Duncan to reply.

"I can give you a few moments before we have tea." He turned and addressed the butler. "MacArthur, can you have tea served in…" he looked at his sister. "Twenty minutes?" She nodded. "Dair and I will be in the study."

The two gentlemen went to the study and she and Glenna went upstairs as did many of the servants, who were loaded up with their purchases for the day.

On reaching their rooms Glenna with military precision diverted all the packages to the appropriate rooms. It was yet another wonder she had to accept. That Glenna, though eighteen years of age, was a force beyond her years.

She turned to Rachael. "Now my dear sister, please freshen up for I shall knock on your door in a few moments so that we can go downstairs, put our feet up and enjoy a wonderful cup of dark glorious tea." She disappeared into her room and Rachael with a sigh made her way to her own room.

Rachael was happy to have a few moments of peace. She took off her travelling boots and sat on her bed. She laid back and closed her eye. She heard the door open and thought that Glenna had entered.

"Just give me a few more minutes, Glenna."

"You can have as much time as you want, my dear."

It was Duncan. She smiled but kept her eyes closed.

"Thank you, kind sir."

Duncan sat at the foot of her bed and lifting her feet. He placed them on his lap.

"Alasdair has gone to stay with a friend. He does not approve of our match."

Rachael pulled herself up into a sitting position but kept her feet on Duncan's lap. "But he is your brother. I do not want to be the cause of your fighting." He sighed and looked at her intently.

"You are not. This has been brewing for some time. He believes he could do a better job of being laird and I happen to agree with him, but I will not tell him that. He has done all he can to help me accept the position that father left me in. But my decision to marry you goes against the way he thinks, the way in which we have been brought up. He sees that you will now take his place and that does not make him happy. I will see him in a few days when he has calmed himself. Then we will talk again. We will work things through. Do not fret."

Rachael had her doubts, but she smiled at Duncan. She was not as sure that things would be right. She looked into his green eyes and was thankful that he had chosen her but she worried about the future. He frowned.

"But there is something that I wish to discuss with you."

Rachael laid down on the bed again. She was not sure she wanted to hear but then he could be joking with her. She closed her eyes and waited.

"And what would that be?"

"Our sleeping arrangements." Rachael opened her eyes and gave her love a *'what are you talking about'* look. He continued with a broader smile than she was comfortable with.

"I agree to wait till we are married back at the castle, but you are my betrothed and I want to be with you and that means at night. Let us consider ourselves hand fasted."

"But Duncan, is that appropriate? This time is so formal. If anyone finds out..."

"It is for me. Hand fasting means we have made a promise and that we can live as husband and wife. It is an old custom, I grant you, but one I am prepared to put in place. I have told MacArthur that we are to be married and that the servants are to start addressing you as if you were already my wife. I think that you will begin to notice the change."

"This is all going so quickly. How can you be sure I am the one for you? I hated you but days ago."

"But you do not hate me now, do you?"

"No. I know its nuts, but I love you more than I can say."

Duncan got up and placed her feet on the bed and came to sit beside her. He put his hand gently on her hair and stroked it.

"You are the one. I have no doubts. Do you doubt our love?"

"No. I have never felt so connected to a person in all my life. We are meant for each other. I'm just feeling that this has happened more quickly than it should."

"Then my dear, do not doubt again and enjoy the wonderful life that we will share together. Time is of no matter to me. I want you."

She smiled but, in her heart, she was crying. She knew that her love for him would not diminish but she was unsure of his love. He declared it stronger than she had heard from anyone before. Would he love her forever? She did not know. Hand fasting was convenient for him and would allow them to sleep together. Not that they did much sleeping. Something in her heart told her that he was but infatuated. She didn't want to believe that. She tried to shake that feeling but it hung around at the back of her mind and made her doubt.

TOURISM?

T*uesday 13ᵗʰ August 1822*

It was late in the evening when he came to her. He escorted her to his room, and they made love with such passion that she thought that they would self-combust. He held her close and continued to whisper his fealty to her. Was this the reason she was sent to 1822? To find her real love and enjoy a future together in the past? She gave up trying to make sense of it and just enjoyed what time she had. Time. What time did she have?

Before dawn she returned to her room. There she slept for a short time. The maid woke her with her usual cup of tea, and she sat in the chair near the window thinking about what today would hold for them. It was cloudy outside and it had rained during the night. She slowly dressed, with the maid's help.

The door opened and the happy and glowing face of Glenna appeared.

"What is bothering you Rachael? Have you had cod liver oil instead of your morning '*Cuppa*'? Did I say that correctly?"

"Yes, you said it correctly. Glenna, can I ask you a question?"

"Most definitely. What is it that concerns you?"

"Duncan is right. You do have a way of reading the thoughts of those you observe. I'm scared. I'm in the past and I have fallen in love with your brother. But will the fairies allow me to stay? I do not want to one day wake up and find myself in the future without Duncan. I couldn't bear it. Do you understand?"

"My poor wee girl. The fae do not play games with those that are true. History has proven that. When we get back to Castle Buin, I will show you our family history and the stories of those who have had similar experiences to you in the fairy circle. This is a gift for you and Duncan. You both must sort out what you want. Each other? Or to be apart? To be here or to return to your future? Yer kin?" She sat in the other chair next to the window. She picked up Rachael's hand and gave it a squeeze.

Rachael gave her head a shake. "You are at peace with this whereas I am not. Duncan believes I'm from the future. I don't doubt that. But you have heard him. He does not believe in the fairies."

"From what I have read neither did the others until they could no longer deny it. Duncan has perhaps a little further to go than you. But all will be right. Trust me. Enjoy the time at the king's celebrations and then discuss it with Duncan when we return home. All will be well."

Rachael wanted to believe her but was sure that Duncan would not. To start to believe in fairies after denying them all his life. Where would that leave her? She finished her 'cuppa' and they went down to breakfast.

Duncan watched her glide into the breakfast room. She was magical, elegant and the most beautiful woman of his acquaintance. And she was his. She came and sat next to him and she placed her hand on his knee briefly. He loved that she wished to touch him when they met. To acknowledge him. It was not the 'done' thing he knew but he loved that of her. She would be guided by her own thinking and behaviour. Perhaps that was a custom of the future and he would enjoy with her.

"I do hope you both slept well?" He asked casually. Rachael looked at him and smiled.

"Yes, thank you."

"I think we will be staying in today as it is raining. The king is due in harbour tomorrow."

"It is all very exciting." Glenna responded. "My maid said they had a procession down near the palace yesterday. That would explain why it was not as crowded, when we were shopping, as we thought it would be."

"Poor Scott. He is going to be very disappointed if it rains the whole time the king is here. None of his plans will come to fruition."

"I remember some of the planned events and if I remember rightly, the rain does not prevent many of the Scottish public coming to see their king. I know that the king was very excited at the warmth of the welcome."

"Well then, he probably will never meet me. I can hardly say that I am excited about his coming."

"Oh, brother, you do fuss so. The king will be happy. Then perhaps things might improve."

"He will not stop the clearing of the highlands. Of that I am sure. Sheep are becoming more important than the people."

"No, he won't stop it. But Duncan, can you not afford to buy some of the lands around you and continue to use the land the way you wish?" He looked at her and marvelled at the ease at which she spoke. Her interest in his clan and the political situation she knew that he hated.

"Tell me Rachael, are there still big landed properties in the future."

"Yes, some but they will diversify into other things. Tourism will become a major earner for the country in my time."

"Tourism? What is that?" Glenna shook her head, finding difficulty in the word.

"I mentioned Victoria before. She will become Queen in 1837. She and her husband love Scotland and Albert will build a castle for his queen. Because they love it here others will come to see what is so wonderful about Scotland. In my time many will come and holiday here. I was one of them."

"So, you suggest that we buy up land around us and use it for 'tourism'?" By now Duncan had turned his chair to face her.

"Yes. I don't know when it all takes off exactly but if you can save your clan by advancing your holdings then why not? You can still run whatever you run, sheep etc. and keep your clan employed."

"It is true that the Grants' wish to rid themselves of the village. Our clan uses it more than they." He wondered what she would make of that remark.

"Then get it. There are places in Aberlour that will prosper. The distillery, the shortbread factory, the tours of the area, canoeing on the Spey. And fishing. Fishing is really popular. I'm sure with a bit of time I can think of other things that have blossomed in my future." Everyone paused to think on what Rachael had said. He more than most. Can knowing the future of the area, help them to keep the things of the past that they enjoy and want?

"After breakfast let us retire to my study so that we can make notes of the possibilities. And I will write to Grant immediately and offer for the village." He could not remove the smile from his face. This information alone would benefit his family. He wanted to drag Rachael away and thank her properly but that would have to wait.

"May I join you?" Glenna added. "I have some ideas and Rachael might be aware if they work."

"It is settled then." Duncan looked out of the window to the grey dark sky and the rain that steadily washed the streets.

"On a day like today, we have a wonderful future to discuss. Perhaps a silver lining might be seen by the Murray clan, despite the greyness of the day."

He smiled at Rachael. Perhaps this was the reason she was brought here? That the fae would use her to save his clan? He wanted to do what he could for the clan but as a man of intelligence and enlightenment could he believe, even for a moment, that the fae were real and were trying to help his clan? That would require much more thought and belief on his part.

It was later in the morning and the rain had not let up. Rachael stood at the library window and looked out onto the street in front of the house and Charlotte Square. The rain still fell and gave no sign of clearing. Even the windows of the houses in the square showed the signs of others who were indoors.

"My dear, come and have a 'cuppa'." She turned and came to the lounge where Glenna sat holding a teacup out toward her. She took it and sat next to her.

"Well, those are my suggestions and I think that the two main ones are the distillery and the shortbread factory. I know some time in the next few years an Act of Parliament will allow you to distil whisky legally for a small fee and that will allow the distillers to grow all over Scotland. The best whisky in the world comes from Scotland."

Duncan laughed. "We could have told you that. I think then

with the town and other lands we can start to head in that direction. We can grow more barley."

"I went to the distillery and I remember that barley wasn't only used by Aberlour but wheat and rye. Does that make sense?"

"Wheat and rye. Good, that will be what we grow as well. We have tried both crops and they do well in the valley. But we will also grow potatoes and vegetables as you have suggested to help us feed our own people. If they grow them for themselves and the castle for now, we might then be able to expand to other areas."

Rachael pondered what she had shared. She could see that Duncan was watching her carefully, not pressing to get more information but allowing her to share what she thought was best. He also had a pencil and wrote down some notes in a book, as they spoke.

"Can I clarify your other holdings? Where else do you make your money on the estate?" She stood and began to pace the room. Deep in thought.

"That would be our imports. But we can export the whisky in time if things go as you say. We import mainly cottons and silks from India. Our clan has done that for some years. We go for the more prestigious weaves. Tea and other items from China, is what we also import but in much smaller quantities. We wish to get involved in other ventures as well. We keep a close eye on the East India Trading company."

Rachael stopped pacing, bowed her head, and closed her eyes. History had always been an area she had loved to read and study. She had already incorporated so much of it into her books. She started pacing again.

"Yes, tea from India is a good move. Perhaps in five or ten years. But keep up China for now. They will make it difficult, but India will eventually do very well with tea. Forget cotton materials. England will be able to produce better quality oh but concentrate on the silks you're importing." She stopped and looked at Duncan. "Do you look after that side of the business?"

"No that is our brother, Hamish. Grandfather had a small import business that father expanded. Hamish was sixteen and had a passion for the business. So, father allowed him to learn from his overseer. When father died, Hamish was happy to run the business for me. It belongs to all the Murray clan not just our family. Hamish has great knowledge and ideas. We can pass this on to him. He should be arriving sometime today. He wants to meet you."

"That is concerning. I really don't want another brother against me. Perhaps we should wait?"

"No need. I don't doubt that Hamish will love you as I do. He is quiet but he will see the blessing that you are to me and the clan."

She smiled at her love and then closed her eyes again to continue to think. MacArthur entered the room.

"Master Hamish has arrived, my laird."

Hamish came in behind the butler and Rachael was again amazed at the characteristics that this family displayed in each of the siblings. Hamish was tall, probably taller than his brother Duncan. Well dressed, with striking carrot red hair. All she could think of was carrot tops as she smiled at him. In fact, she remembered the painting of Duncan's parents and saw in Hamish a younger version of his father.

He bowed toward Rachael and she curtseyed. Then he went to Duncan and heartily hugged him, slapping him on the back. Duncan's greeting was just as hearty.

"So good that you have arrived in Edinburgh, brother. I have plenty of news to tell you." His accent was deep and very Scottish. Not at all anglicised as Duncan and Alasdair's who had studied in England.

He then went to Glenna, picking her up and swinging her around. Glenna's high-pitched squeal revealed a deep joy she shared with this brother. He finally put her down and kissed her flushed cheek.

"You are more beautiful every day, sis. We will be beating the men from your door."

He placed his hands on his hips and it was then that Rachael noticed that he wore the traditional kilt. Not the kilt that Scott had been promoting but the mass of material wrapped and belted around the body. It took her breath away. It suited him to his core. She could not imagine him in the clothes of his brother Duncan.

He stood there with his gaze firmly fixed on her. He was taking her measure. She waited patiently with a quick look at Duncan and then Glenna.

"You, my dearie, must be Rachael. I can see why my brother has fallen in love with yee. I know my sister and brother well and if they welcome you into this strange but wonderful family, then so do I."

He came over and Rachael was worried he would pick her up and start swinging her around. But he stopped in front of her, bowed and lifted her right hand and kissed her fingers. Ever so gently.

"Just you remember brother, dear, she is mine." Then Duncan laughed and soon everyone joined in. Duncan placed his arm around Rachael's waist and whispered into her ear. "You have another supporter, my love."

MacArthur re-entered the room and announced luncheon. Rachael looked outside the window as they headed to the dining room. It was still pouring with rain.

Over the afternoon she remained in discussion with Duncan and Hamish about the plans that she suggested they make. He liked the whisky idea and did not hesitate to believe her that the laws in Scotland would soon change. He agreed with all the suggestions. He wished for the family to come to the old house that they had always used when visiting Edinburgh but with thanks Duncan declined. His aunt's home was closer to all the events that would be occurring with the king's visit and that provided them with an easier base.

They discussed modernising the old family home and Hamish agreed on the condition that Rachael had her hand in the décor.

"I only stay in the place for short periods. I am often travelling on business. And now with your suggestions I plan to travel a bit more. You will need the house when coming to the city."

"I had no idea that you had another house. I just assumed you stayed here with your aunt."

"The house is closer to the bay. In fact, it is on the other side of the Forth. Quieter and allows us to get home more easily. So, what do you say?" Hamish looked at her expectantly.

She looked into the eyes of the newest family member. And how could she not agree? "I will agree but that the house is used by the whole family. Agreed?" She looked at Duncan and Glenna and they both nodded.

"I am so delighted for you and Duncan though I don't think he deserves yee, yee ken?' He came to stand before her and again taking her hand in his, lifting it and kissed her fingers. "I will be telling Alasdair that also. The man has a boulder for a brain."

"He went to stay with you, did he?" Duncan asked. A frown upon his face.

"Yes, but I told him from the beginning that it is your decision who yee marry not his."

"Very wise Hamish. I trust you will confirm to him they are my thoughts too." Added Glenna.

"I think that he is aware. He is troubled. He will recover from his malady. I suggest that you allow him time for his brain to catch up with him. Boulders take time to move. Now if you will excuse me."

And just like that he was gone.

"Your brother is a delight and I am glad to know him."

"He is very much like our father, both in looks and in manners. I am sure our father would have loved you as much as I do."

Rachael could feel the warmth reach her face, but she was content. This was the man she loved. Now all she needed to do was be at peace, living in her past. She needed to talk with Duncan of her concerns, but she would wait till they returned to Castle Buin.

<hr>

The evening showed no sign of the rain stopping. The day indoors was refreshing despite all the discussions and plans that were made.

The king was due to arrive in the city tomorrow and all were excited despite the rain. But Duncan had no intention of going into the old town if it were raining.

"Rain in Edinburgh is bad enough, but these downpours will be washing a great deal of dirt and muck around the city. I am not sure I want to be in it. And you, dear ladies, most definitely will not."

Rachael rose from her seat. "That we can worry about tomorrow. Right now, I'm off to bed." She headed to the door and turned to say goodnight. Both Duncan and Glenna had stood.

"I agree. A wonderful day we have had but my bed is calling me." Glenna shot past Rachael. "Goodnight." She called as she dashed up the stairs.

"I will fetch you shortly." Duncan's penetrating stare held her to the spot. He walked to her side, leaned over, and kissed her. He sighed. "Oh, how I need your kisses."

She smiled and leant forward and kissed his nose. Then descended to his lips and nibbled them ever so lightly.

"I need not only your kisses." She turned and went to the stairs. Looking back, she could see his gaze drift over her body. He took her meaning and smiled with such intent that she was sure he would have taken her there and then had she not continued up the stairs.

NOT TODAY YOUR HIGHNESS

W*ednesday 14th August 1822*

The new day had brought more rain. The sky was dark and so was
Rachael's mood. She tried to explain to Duncan that where she
lived the sun shone most of the time and that rain when it came
was quick and then gone. The greyness of the past days was not
what she was used to, and this played havoc with her mind. It made
her second guess all her thoughts. He said that he understood but
again the darkness of her mood, doubted that he did.

One of the servants was sent to the bay to keep an eye out for
the king and find out the time he was planning to disembark. But
the rain continued through the day. Finally, in the afternoon the
servant returned with the news that the king had indeed arrived in
the Firth of Forth at around noon but that the landing was post-
poned till the morrow due to the torrential rain.

This suited them all. Duncan had a letter to write regarding the
purchasing of the village and wanted to get it to the Grant's as soon

as he could. Rachael wanted to nap. Her evenings had been well occupied with Duncan. She hoped the nap would lift her flat spirits. But she also wanted to take stock of her new dresses that had arrived that morning, newly altered or made for her.

"Rachael, they are beautiful. You will be the belle at the ball. Red is just so becoming on you."

"You don't think that it is too provocative? I do not wish to embarrass Duncan."

"You will never do that I can assure you. Your beauty and your love for Duncan will win most of the chieftains over. Actually, I will tell you later of a few gentlemen that you might wish to avoid. For they will try to have you for themselves." She laughed and Rachael's mood lightened listening to her.

"I will wear the red dress to the Grand Ball and wear the turquoise silk to the levee. Can't believe that I will be attending a levee. Are you sure that I will be able to attend?"

"Most definitely. You are Duncan's future lady so you will be expected to be there. As his sister, I too can attend so you will not be alone. A friend of mine will also be there, Delia Farraday. You will like her. She was known to us first as Delia Fitzgibbon. But there is a very detailed story behind the change of name. But for now, you should know that she will be your friend and understand your mixed and confused feelings. Probably more than most young ladies."

Rachael sat with her notepad in hand and stopped to look at her friend.

"What makes you so sure?"

"Simple. Her life has been full of scandal. She believed for some time that she was a child of uncertain parentage, and that the father she had known all her life was in fact not her father. She ran away, to stay with a distant relative. But now she is reunited with the man who she loved as her father all her life. She has chosen to stay in Scotland rather than return to Kent. That is what I mean. She has heartaches but she loves Scotland and I believe she will like you."

Rachael listened as she continued to tell of her friend and her desire to stay in Scotland. It was a wonderful story and Rachael was looking forward to meeting her in person. Rachael imagined she could turn the story into a wonderful book if she were back home. Having a pencil had enabled her to make clearer and better notes.

"There is one other point that you should know. I think that she is in love with my brother."

"Duncan? Oh no."

"No not Duncan, Alasdair." Rachael gave a sigh of relief.

"Oh. And is Alasdair in love with her?"

"Not yet but he will be."

"You seem so sure."

"Yes, I do. I know them both and they suit each other very well. I think that the time is right for them to get together. I'm sure that with you and Duncan getting together, Alasdair will be more inclined to listen to his heart."

"You're a little match maker, aren't you?"

Rachael was amused at the meddling Glenna was undertaking. She would be happy to see Alasdair happy as she was happy with Duncan. At that moment she stopped, closed her eyes, and tried to picture Duncan's face. It came easily. His green eyes and his black hair. She imagined running her hands through his hair and pictured his delighted face as he stared into her eyes. All her doubts suddenly disappeared. This is what she wanted.

Past, future be damned.

Rachael stood. She looked at Glenna. "I'm sorry but I must speak with Duncan"

"Of course. Go. He is in the study."

She left the room rather quickly and was sorry to dash away from Glenna as she had. But the urge to speak with Duncan became immediate. She noted that no more man servants were waiting and watching her.

When had they stopped?

Coming down the stairs, she passed one of the maids.

"Morning Miss. Did you know that Master Alasdair is in the study with the laird?"

"No, I was unaware Grace. I was just on my way to the study. Has Master Alasdair been with the laird for long?"

"No miss. He has just arrived. Mr MacArthur suggested that I let you and Miss Glenna know that he was here."

"Thank you, Grace. Please go up and let Miss Glenna know."

Rachael sat on the step reluctant to go any further. She had no desire to hear the two men fight again. From where she sat, she could hear their voices but with a sigh of relief they did not appear to be yelling at each other. Moments later Grace descended the stairs and passed Rachael on her way back down to the kitchens. Then Glenna sat down beside her.

"Have you heard any raised voices?" she whispered.

"No. But he has only just arrived."

Glenna took her hand and gave it a squeeze. "Do not fret. I have no doubt that Alasdair will see sense. Just be patient."

"Do you have fairy blood? You seem so sure of things."

Glenna laughed.

"The truth is easy to see for those who look for it."

"You're a real little philosopher, aren't you?"

Glenna chuckled quietly.

The two young ladies sat waiting to see if anything would happen. After about fifteen minutes, MacArthur came to the study door and entered. In moments he came back out and headed for the stairs. Rachael stood and waited for him to come to the landing.

"The laird has asked you to come to the library, Miss Rachael."

"Thank you, MacArthur."

She turned and looked at Glenna. Come down in five minutes, would you? Just in case I need a friend."

"You'll be fine. But yes, I will, in five minutes."

———

She knocked ever so quietly and heard Duncan's voice.

"Come."

She entered the room reluctantly.

"Rachael, my dear. You do not need to knock. This is your home at least for now."

As she closed the door behind her, the two gentlemen stood. Duncan put his hand out toward her, and she slowly made her way to him, trying not to look at Alasdair. Her hands were cold and she noticed that she was trembling. She looked at Duncan and his demeanour seemed relaxed. She kept her head down as she waited quietly next to the man she loved.

"Rachael."

It was Alasdair who spoke. She looked at him. He was dressed well but was soaked to the skin. Her fear vanished, concerned for his welfare.

"Alasdair, you will catch your death if you remain in those wet clothes. I do wish you would go upstairs and change."

"I will Rachael. But first I wish to apologise."

"Accepted. Now please go and change?"

"Rachael. Not just for my behaviour but for my disbelief. After talking with Hamish, I realised that I had judged you wrong. Strange things happen in this world and I should have accepted the truth you told. From the beginning you promised you would tell the truth, but I would not believe you."

"I understand. I would probably not believe you if you were in my place. But I appreciate the apology very much."

She went over and hugged him. He tried to push her away as he was wet, but she would not be moved.

"Let me go Rachael so that I can get out of these wet clothes. I will stay home. Please be assured that I will not doubt you again."

He left the room. She turned to look at Duncan.

"I am proud of you, my love." He opened his arms wide.

Rachael came over to him and hugged him as if she would never let him go. He pulled her away from him.

"Now stand here near the fire to dry off, unless you wish to change."

"No, I am fine. It is but a little damp. It will dry off soon enough. I wanted to talk to you before I found out that Dair had returned. Can we talk now? I will sit near the fire while we chat."

"Of course, my dear. What is concerning you?"

She took in a deep breath and gazed into her beloved's eyes. "That's the thing. Nothing is concerning me. I was just upstairs when I suddenly realised that I wanted to be only with you. No matter what happens. So long as we are together. What I mean to say is…"

"You have no doubts?"

"That's right. I'm sure, very sure that this is right. I can't understand why all of you have so readily accepted me and believe what I have said is true."

"Because it is true." Duncan sat on the chair opposite her.

"I know." She smiled and breathed in. It had felt as if she had been holding on to her breath for days. "I love you, Duncan. I think that I always have and that I always will."

He got up and went to her, leaning down and gently touched her lips with his. Then he drew her into his arm and deepened the kiss. He explored her mouth slowly with his tongue tasting her lips. She adored his kisses. Cool, a hint of whisky as she supped. He wanted her again. His body could not hide it from her. He slowed the exploration and withdrew from her mouth. She felt the loss keenly.

"I would like to continue with this but not here."

She leaned her forehead against his chest keeping her arms around him.

"I too. I think that we will be disturbed here."

As she spoke Glenna came into the room.

"Later brother. Leave the poor girl alone." She smiled at Duncan with mischief in her eyes. Rachael was now glad that she had asked her friend to come in. It could have been embarrassing if their kissing had continued much longer.

Duncan lowered his head and kissed Rachael on the forehead.

"I think it is time to get ready for supper. We have plans for tomorrow whether it rains, or it shines."

Duncan looked at his family that now included his Rachael. He was content but still was unsure he wanted the role of laird. Having that position had never been right. Even now with Rachael at his side he was unsure. Not of her but his position. But at least he now knew the doubts that Rachael had envisaged were gone. And that pleased him. He still had lingering doubts though he had no desire to share that with Rachael. The desire, no the need to be with her was over-powering. Having known her for only days he could not explain it. Perhaps his heart would relax in time. Time.

He still had suspicions of Rachael's story because the enlightened man within him could not imagine the scenario. But then he remembered the stories that had come through the family for generations. Could he push them completely away? After all it would seem they were true. He only needed to feel her body beneath him to know she loved him in truth. But her story still disturbed him.

He would not think on it now. The next few weeks with the king's visit they would be distracted and then they could all go home. Perhaps then his future and hers would become clearer.

———

Rachael could see that Duncan was deep in thought as he looked around at his family. Family. Now she was part of this family and was very excited at the thought. There would definitely be things that she would miss from the future but as she looked around the room in which she sat she also knew that she was lucky to be part of a wealthy family in this time. Duncan disturbed her thoughts. But a disturbance that she wanted.

"I would like to share some of the plans for the next few weeks." Everyone turned to face Duncan as he pulled a paper from inside his evening jacket.

"The king will be disembarking from his ship the Royal George regardless of the weather, tomorrow. Scott will not allow any more delays." He gave a little chuckle. "Hamish, Dair and I will join the king's procession from the quay to the city. A three-mile curricle ride. Ladies, I would prefer you stay here especially as the weather may yet be inclement."

He looked at Alasdair and continued.

"We will meet Hamish at the Anchor Inn around eleven and wait for news as to the king disembarking. Then we will ride in an open curricle, you and me in the front and Hamish on the luggage rack, into the city, behind the king. The king will receive the key to the city, and then we will return home. Hamish will return with us here for dinner and plans to stay here until the king leaves Edinburgh."

"It will be wonderful to have all the family together." Glenna smiled at Rachael. "All the family."

"Most assuredly." Alasdair agreed.

Rachael looked at Alasdair and the twinkle in his eyes had returned. She loved him as a brother and now realised that the feelings she had for Dair were the same as she had held for Josh. A platonic love. She gave him a smile and received a beaming one from him in return.

"Friday is a day of rest for the king. He will be staying at the Castle of Dalkeith. In the evening, Scott has arranged an evening of 'Illumination' in the new town. I am not sure what that entails but we will attend. We will be walking down. If it rains the event will be shifted to another evening, I imagine. We will have to wait and see."

"My, this is exciting. I remember reading about some of these events." Rachael had been so very quiet most of the evening but suddenly all eyes were fixed on her. And for the first time she saw anticipation in their expressions and not suspicion. She closed her eyes in her usual manner to think and tried to remember some of the items.

"It will rain tomorrow but only in the morning. So, wear a raincoat, gentlemen." She lifted her gaze and fixed it on Duncan. Then she smiled at them all and they chuckled. She closed her eyes again.

"As for the illuminations…The Duke of Athol is in town. He will love the event. He will sit in a window of his house and watch the lights go out. At least that is what I remember from my history book. The Grant girls will see the glow over the new town as they come back from the country. 'Glowing with incandescent fire'."

"Do you know the Grant girls?" Alasdair asked.

"No. How could I? We haven't been here that long, and I don't think we have met any Grants?" She looked from Duncan to Glenna and back again as they shook their heads.

"No, we have not." Duncan grinned at her. "But you will be pleased to know that Athol has a house here in Charlotte Square." He got up from the table and took her hand and brought her to the dining room window. It looked out over the Square. "Over there."

He pointed in the direction of a house across the square. And I believe that he has a very good view of the new town and George Street from his windows."

He kissed her on the forehead, and they returned to their seats.

"Tell me," asked Alasdair, "How do you remember this part of our history?"

Rachael looked at him then to Glenna and finally to Duncan. "In my time I wrote stories. Stories that we call romances." The heat was rising to her face again. She gave her head a little shake. She was proud of her writing and pulled herself straight in her chair. "My last story was set in Edinburgh at the time of this event. So, I have read a lot about what the king did. History is a passion of mine as is Scotland. I am hopeful I might be able to remember things as we go along."

All eyes remained fixed on her. She knew by their expressions that she could tell them that the moon was made of blue cheese and they would trust her. But she had no intention of leading them astray. She wanted their trust. Always.

"Then if you remember anything that may be useful please tell me." Duncan smiled at her and she could see the sincerity in his eyes. This is what she desired. A relationship that would make a difference in each other's lives as well as in the lives of others.

"I will be meeting the king on Saturday with a number of other lairds. But that will be me alone." He looked at Rachael and smiled. "We will eat together that evening and can sort out the rest of the week's activities then. I hope that is sufficient for now?"

"Of course, Duncan." Glenna pattered her brother's hand. "It is so very exciting. But for me I just plan to have fun and a little excitement. I have invited Delia to join us here on Friday and to walk with us into the new town for the Illuminations."

Alasdair's face lit up. So, a spark of interest was there. Could he too be happy?

"It will be wonderful to see her again." He said. "I am surprised that she did not return to her father in Kent after they were reconciled."

"Are you not?" Glenna added and gave him a knowing look. "She loves Scotland and wished to be away from the excitement of London. But now she gets to see the king anyway. Perhaps the king pursues her?" Glenna laughed.

"I look forward to meeting her." Rachael looked at them both. "I feel I already know her; you have mentioned her so many times."

"As for me," Duncan added, "I have a great deal of paperwork that must be done, so every chance I get I will be in my study. I do not want to see the king but will have too." Rachael could see as he was still very unhappy that the king was here. But he looked at her longingly and she knew their evening trysts would not be affected.

"Well my dear family...that sounds weird, doesn't it?" Rachael announced as she stood up from the table. "I plan to get some well needed sleep. After all it is not every day that a future girl gets to meet a king." She curtsied and headed to the door. She turned and started to laugh. She watched as each one of them laughed with her. This was her family.

"I thought you would never come to me." Rachael said as Duncan led her into the room.

He quietly closed the door to his bedroom, glad that he had Rachael alone with him at last. This was much more important than business.

"I must apologise, my dear. But Hamish and Alasdair had a number of matters that needed to be dealt with tonight." He came over and took her into his arm. His passion filled kiss lasted several minutes. He wanted to show her that he would rather have had been with her than doing business.

"If you continue to kiss me like that, I promise you will never hear any complaints from me again. Nor will I let you out of my sight."

He picked her up and carried her to his bed. Slowly he undid the buttons of her nightdress. He gently pulled them apart to reveal the breasts that he had thought about all night. He reached down to sup on them, each in turn. This beautiful delicate flesh belonged to him and nothing would keep him from her. She meowed her pleasure deep in her chest. That glorious chest.

He was ready to take her but wanted to give her more pleasure before having his way. He explored other areas of her body, looking, feeling, manipulating, and tugging. The pleasure for her she did not keep silent, which only made him search for other areas of her body that he could please.

"Oh, Duncan please come inside me before I scream the place down."

Her expressions delighted him, and he laughed at the frustration in her voice. He got off her and removed all his clothes as she removed her nightdress. Then he was on top of her again supping on her breasts and making her moan even louder than before. Finally, he thrust himself deep inside her and she did scream her joy into his kiss. Back and forth as she came into the rhythm with him. They danced their beautiful dance and went sailing into the sky above them and met their release together in the stars.

They lay holding each other as they slowly made their way back to his bed in the here and now. He would rather remain in the stars with her sailing beyond this world. But he knew they could only seek out moments like this for now and that was enough for him.

He held her close as she whispered, "Promise you will love me like that forever."

"I will my darling. Forever." he replied as they fell asleep in each other's arms.

WELCOME TO EDINBURGH

*T*hursday 15*th* August 1822

Rachael was right again. It was raining. Being in a curricle with this weather was most uncomfortable. But she was right about the rain. However wet, even he was surprised at how many folks had come to see the king in the flesh. But on cue the clouds parted, and the rain ceased as the king's barge came to the dock. Pipers played; the Royal Standard flew from the lighthouse tower. Ceremony took hold and Scott was beaming with pride.

The king disembarked and met many of the dignitaries including Duncan. Flags were flying and several bands were playing the national anthem. Duncan smiled, amazed at all the pomp. But the joyous occasion was soon shattered as the king sat in his open carriage.

Laird Glengarry dressed in his plaid and bonnet and looking very much like the Scots of Culloden, rode up at pace on his horse, swept off his bonnet and cried aloud, "Your highness is welcomed to Scotland." The king graciously bowed to Glengarry as his carriage moved off. No offence was taken at the unexpected intrusion, but Scott gave Glengarry a look that showed his displeasure in abundance. Duncan laughed. It would seem that Scott would not get his way in all things.

Duncan continued to chuckle to himself as he saw the crowd's reaction. All were pleased with Glengarry's performance. He only wished he had thought of it. But he also appreciated the king's patience with the old laird. After all, not all wished his highness to be here. He was but one.

It was a slow ride to the city and the king appeared to be enjoying himself. Duncan had enough glimpses of him as he rode in the third carriage behind the king. His highness was constantly waving, as the crowds clung to the cobbled curbs as he passed. He paid particular attention to where many of the women were gathered.

The rumours of his womanising could be right. They adore him. And he adored them.

All levels of society were present, mingled together and triumphant that their king had come to visit with them. They hoorayed his passing and then followed the procession of carriages and vehicles as they entered the city. Snake like, it made its way to Picardy Place where a mock gate to the city had been erected. Again, he marvelled and shook his head at the details Scott had taken with the procession. The man had created a unique experience for the king and his subjects.

Sir Patrick Walker and Mr Tait, the deputy Lord Lyon advanced on the mock gateway as the carriage pulled up. Sir Patrick lifted his white rod and struck the gate three times. It immediately opened and the king's carriage came through the gateway.

The king rose to his feet as the carriage paused. He bowed to the crowd who hooted and hoorayed. William Arbuthnot came over to the king and handed him the keys to the city. The king lifted them from the red satin cushion and held them in the air. More hurrays followed. Then he placed them back on the cushion with great ceremony and announced that they 'were in no better hands than the Lord Provost and the magistrates of the fair city.'

Interesting. He had not expected that.

Duncan looked into each of the Scotsman faces that were near him and saw admiration.

Disturbing.

Each step and detail were becoming etched into his mind. He wanted to tell Rachael and his sister all the details. Even if he could not believe them himself.

The procession went on growing in number as the crowds and more carriages joined the throng. The king entered Prince Street. The crowds were gathered on Carlton Hill and the smoke was rising from the summit as the artillery guns were fired in welcome. Duncan heard the king's remarks every now and then when his carriage grew close. "How superb" and "My God, how fine this is." The king seemed to be truly enjoying the experience. At one point he saw the king looking down from the summit onto the golden capped turrets of Holyrood Palace. Then looking at the crowds around him. He seemed visibly moved by the expressions of loyalty by the crowds on the hill.

More speeches were made from the summit but finally the king left for Dalkeith. The crowds lingered as did the triumphant mood.

Duncan and his brothers though now dry from the early morning shower went back to the town house in New Town looking forward to a warm drink and a rest from the ceremonies that they had been made to be a part of. Duncan was amazed at the king's welcome and said so. He was disturbed at how well the king had behaved and how the crowds had adored him. None of that was what he had expected. Perhaps this king was not the overlord as other kings had been. Perhaps the Scots could be recognised as the men and women that they really were. Full blooded scots. This king still had a lot to prove if he wanted his loyalty. But he had to admit that he was impressed.

———

"How exciting. But tell me is he as fat, dare I say it, as the papers say that he is?" Glenna's excitement could not be curbed. Neither could hers for that matter. They had been waiting patiently for the brothers to return to feed them all about the events they had witnessed. And they did not disappoint.

"He was in his army uniform. Full regalia for his position as the head of the army. His weight was obvious but then he is a very tall man, so he carries it better than most." Duncan was trying to be diplomatic; she could tell. Rachael watched him carefully, noting the change in tone as he now addressed the king. So different from the comments that he had made back at the castle. Even this morning at breakfast.

"So, dear brother, you are saying that he carries his weight well?" Glenna continued.

"Well not exactly. But...well enough." This brought laughter from them all. "He was gracious and extremely well received. The crowds amazed me. I had not imagined so many would come out to see him. Along the whole route people lined the streets six or seven deep. Children sitting on shoulders of parents and adults who were happy to oblige."

Rachael continued to smile. Perhaps the change in attitude to royalty began here with Duncan. History might not be the big mystery that she had envisaged for so many years.

———

Later as they dined together Duncan again watched his family all together. He smiled at each member and especially at Rachael. He believed that nothing could drive the tranquillity away. But the doubts that he had been harbouring were again rising to the surface of his mind. Rachael gave no indication that she was lying so why did it keep raising up in his mind? He frowned and pushed the thoughts away again and again.

He watched as they spoke together. Even Alasdair was back to his usual self. But he wanted to be alone with Rachael. He wanted to gain more information about the future Scotland that she said was a place she loved. Her love for his homeland was clear. Her eyes shone when she talked about it. She did not lie. But they shone also when she talked about the king. The king. Was there something going on there? No of course not. She loved him. But it was a pride, a loyalty that she could not hide. Was that wrong?

After some hours they were finally laying together in his bed. They made love first. His need for her was growing. This was the girl, no the woman he would one day have as his wife. But the future, the concept, the actuality, was standing between them. He could not put his trust in myth or folklore. He needed to know more.

"I know about the cars and the motorways. How people will dress and the jobs they will do. Tell me about your job."

Rachael cuddled closer to him and he drew her nearer.

"I am a lawyer."

"But I thought you were a writer?"

"I am. But that is not a fulltime job. I studied to be a lawyer. I work mainly in the field of family law. And that is dealing with the breakdown of people's marriages, care of children and things like that."

"This seems so strange to me that you would bring in the law to deal with people's inner most relationships. Certainly, everyone would want the right things for their children?"

"Well, you are a man of honour and any child of yours, even the females will be taken well care of."

"What do you mean by even the females?"

"Now, here in this time, women have no rights. If a husband dies, the woman will lose everything she knows and loves because she is a female. All will go to the son. Or if not the son then a close male relative. That is unless the man makes certain provisions for his wife."

"But most women will be protected by their families?"

"If that were true, they wouldn't need lawyers. If there is another male who will do what is right, then yes, they will be looked after. My study of the law makes it perfectly clear that women had no rights at this time. If she was rich, her money went to the husband, even though it was given to her. If he dies, she will lose it, if it is not clearly laid out that it is hers and will return to her. My experience says that does not happen very often."

"I see. But why do the women feel they are entitled?" Rachael took in a deep breath. She was holding back her anger. He could tell. What had he said that angered her? She gave a little shake then continued.

"Women in my time often work to raise money for the family to use. But it does not belong to the guy. We do not have servants in the future, well at least not the way you have them now. Women do all the cooking, cleaning, raising the children and stuff like that. Quite often they are working outside the home as well. Like me. I look after people's legal interests. But I have a house of my own and have only me to clean it and maintain it. I do not have staff, servants who can do that for me. If I want it done, I will have to pay for it."

"This world you come from is very confusing."

"Not really."

Rachael yawned and snuggled in a little closer. Her breathing slowed and soon she was asleep in his arms. His thoughts would not allow him to sleep. Dealing with the king was less complicated than trying to work out the world Rachael lived in. Assuming all she said was real and not a dream or her imagination. Why did he still question her? She had given her doubt away. Why did he still cling to it?

ILLUMINATIONS

*F**riday 16th August*

The day was a sombre one. Many in the town felt deflated that the king was not visiting them this day but remaining at Dalkeith. He was enjoying the county pleasures it was said. For Duncan, a visit with the king was planned at Dalkeith. He spent some of the morning at the king's side, at his request. He said little about the visit when he returned but Rachael could see he was reflective. He was quiet and thoughtful. She found it strange after such a short period of time she could work out his moods and demeanour.

Everyone awaited the evening and what Rachael had promised would be an evening of great excitement. The 'illuminations' was to be an event that they and others would talk about for years to come. They had eaten early so that as the sun set, they began their walk into the new town streets.

The first thing Rachael noted was that the streets were filled with people from all levels of the society. Those of high rank to those with no rank at all. People dressed in the finery of the higher classes. Frills and furbelows. Those of lower state such as business and the service industries in their everyday wear. Then the servant classes and finally the lower classes who were not so well dressed nor refined as the upper classes but were just as excited as all the rest to be enjoying the event. She smiled for a moment. The fact the classes could not be defined and sorted so easily in her time. In the future it was harder to tell. She liked that idea. The future had advantages.

The broad pavements of the new town held a moving mass of people whichever way they went. The other thing she noticed was all the houses and businesses got involved. Some very simply with a candlelight in each window of their home. Others had arranged the candles into figures, animal, and human shapes. Even the shape of flowers. No doubt a servant remained in the house to be sure the lighting was not disturbed but Rachael was sure every other body in the city were walking the streets. She listened to the comments from the passers-by. Some innocent and transfixed with what they saw, others found the lighting vulgar or merely advertising.

As the night wore on, she had seen her share of thistles, saltires, cherubs, and stars. Patriotic slogans also wove its way into the presentations. Representations of the king, crown, followers and alike. All had taken her breath away. Even a large bonfire on Arthur's seat continued to burn as the night's activity drew to a close. She saw huge iron baskets filled with glowing coals on the battlements of the great castle. And rockets being fired into the air from the new city. All these events were amazing. Far beyond what she could have imagined.

At ten in the evening there was a thunderous salvo of guns from Calton Hill and Salisbury Craig's. This signalled a closing of the events of the evening. The creativity was marvellous. The lights and the pageantry captured her imagination. Nearly for four hours, she and the others walked around. Little talking had been done as they marvelled at the magical event. She pondered how marvellous it would be if she had a camera to capture these events. Alas that was not to be.

As the night drew to a close, bands of boys appeared with lighted torches to escort groups back to their homes both in the new and old town. She found this final touch remarkable. To organise such a touching finish to the evening. No rank, no favouritism just escorts. Scott and his minions should be most pleased with this event. And his majesty missed the whole thing having deposited himself in Dalkeith to enjoy the country. Their gain and his loss.

"What a remarkable evening." Rachael took off her hat and coat with assistance from Duncan. She smiled into his face. "I'm delighted you had given the servants the night off so they too could enjoy the lights. They must have enjoyed it as much as we."

"You were correct in what you remembered of the history. I had not thought that mere light could make the town look so beautiful." He placed the coats and hats on the stand near the front door.

"It was truly one of the most wonderful evenings I have ever witnessed." Glenna added as she too placed her coat and hat on the stand.

"A remarkable sight." Alasdair concluded. "Now if you will excuse me, I will escort Delia in her carriage back to her home."

He left them all standing in the hall after they had said their goodbyes.

Duncan turned to face all of them. "Sleep well. Tonight, we will have fairy lights dancing before our eyes." Everyone laughed.

Everyone except Glenna. The seriousness of her face told Rachael that she was not amused. But she kept her silence.

"I will be visiting with the king again tomorrow afternoon. At Holyrood. He has summoned me again." Rachael could see a hint of concern in his eyes but that soon disappeared.

"Sleep well." He repeated and headed up the stairs.

With that Rachael went upstairs and everyone went to their rooms. At the top of the stairs, Duncan took Rachael into his arms and kissed her.

"My love, I wish for you to sleep soundly. I need to be up early to make some extra plans for my visit with the king. I will let you sleep alone tonight."

Rachael was surprised but not shocked. Their evenings had been very strenuous, and both lacked full nights of sleep despite the contentment they had also received.

"Very well my dear, but be warned that when we marry, we can still sleep together without the extra activity." She smiled and kissed his nose.

"Believe me, my lady, that will be impossible. With you at my side, in my bed, I would have to taste your sweetness. Every night." He kissed her gently on her lips and went to his room. She turned and headed to her own.

Glenna was waiting for her. "I do not like my brothers, either of them making fun of the fae. They do not understand."

"I thought you were displeased. But what concerns you? Duncan was joking, I'm sure."

"That is the point. More is going on around them than they care to notice. I just wish they would be cautious with what they say. At this moment he shows no belief and that is concerning. If he wants to be with you, he will need to believe."

Rachael could understand her concern but could not explain the underlying feeling she had, that Glenna was not telling her everything. She brushed it aside. She was tired and needed some sleep.

Surely the fae would allow her dream of being with Duncan to come true?

"Don't let their lack of understanding upset you. Now go to your bed and sleep. It has been a long day and a very big evening. The morning will allow us to be fully refreshed to face the coming days."

THE KING

T *uesday 20th August 1822*

The previous days were a blur. Duncan had his coming and goings and she had seen less of him. She understood that things were busy for him. Especially as he had spent even more time with the king than either of them had expected. She did not want to burden him with the schoolgirl feelings she had of always wanting to be near him. She had known that life was going to be busy while in Edinburgh and that is just how things had been.

Today would be a special day. One that she had never hoped she could experience. Delia had arrived early so that Rachael, Glenna, and Delia could have breakfast together and prepare for their visit and presentation to the king at Holyrood. Today was the king's levee. And she still could not stop laughing about it.

"I have seen him with my father in London, but when he was Regent. I have not seen him since and anticipate that now he is king, he has changed a great deal."

"I just find the whole experience exciting." Rachael could not believe her luck, as Duncan's fiancée, she would have the chance to be presented to a man of history. Especially one that she had taken some interest in due to her love of the regency period.

"Well, all I can say is that I hope I do not laugh in his face if I find him somewhat fatter than what Duncan has said of him." With that all three young ladies where found giggling as Duncan came into the room.

He came over to Rachael's chair and placed his hands on her shoulders so that she would not get up. He leant down and kissed the top of her head.

"Greetings ladies." he said as Rachael lifted her eyes to greet him. "I hope that you are all excited at the thought of greeting the king at his levee."

This brought a cacophony of giggles from all three young ladies.

"Now, now, ladies. A few instructions. It is custom, that you must be kissed by the king and so you shall. Be sure you offer him your cheeks and not your mouths. Believe me your mouths will be taken if you do not keep him in check."

"Oh Duncan," Rachael continued to giggle. "If he kisses us then what does he do with all the gentlemen when he meets them at their levee?"

Duncan smiled a cheeky smile at her knowing full well that he had already warned her to stay away from the king's wandering lips. She was jesting with him knowing that the men were greeted with far more respect than the women.

"We promise to behave, brother, but do tell me is the king very fat?" Now Glenna was jesting with her brother knowing the king to be overweight. Duncan continued ignoring the comment by his sister. She had been repeating the question for days.

"We will leave for the palace at noon. The king is due at two o'clock, but the ladies must be in line through the waiting rooms at the palace in order of appearance, as Scott and the king has requested. You, sister, will be presented first, then Rachael followed by Delia. You will curtsy and then the king will kiss you. You will not speak unless the king asks you a question. As there are over four hundred ladies being presented, I doubt that he will speak to anyone. And remember I will be presenting you so do not embarrass the Murray name."

By the time Duncan had finished his speech, the ladies had gathered their demeanours and sat soberly. He bowed and went to the door.

"Be ready to leave by noon." he said as he went out the door.

"Now I am scared, in fact I'm petrified." Rachael said to the others.

Duncan stood at the bottom of the stairs waiting for the ladies to come down. It was noon, just. The carriage was waiting at the front and the door was open. He took his fob watch from his coat and checked the time. He looked at the stairwell to see all three ladies coming down. His sister led the way. She was wearing a new light blue silk gown that she had purchased when they arrived in town. Her hair was beautifully coiffured and had small peacock feathers dropping from the back. She looked older and wiser than her eighteen years.

Delia came next and was a great beauty also. Her features and colouring were very English, but she too was dressed to display the wisdom beyond her years. Finally, his Rachael came. Her turquoise silk hugged her figure and showed off her beautiful eyes. She too had used the peacock feathers but had them hugging her curls as if each feather embraced her hair. She was stunning. He could not take his eyes off her. She would no doubt be the belle of all the ladies presented today. She was grace personified.

Rachael came to stand in front of him. She placed her finger under his chin and closed his mouth. He had no idea that he had been gaping. She smiled her 'I love you' smile at him and he lifted her hand and kissed her fingers.

"Let me escort you ladies to the palace." He offered his arm to Rachael and his sister and Hamish who was also waiting in the foyer offered his arm to Delia.

He helped each lady into the closed carriage. Rachael thanked him for the closed carriage. She was worried the open one would have ruined their hair.

The day was still and clear and slightly warm. The carriage ride did not take more than ten minutes, but they waited in the line-up of carriages for at least twenty. By the time they arrived at the palace doors, the master of ceremonies had all the ladies in order in certain waiting rooms, waiting for the king to arrive.

They waited patiently to be summoned to the line that went before the king. The ladies would be presented by their gentleman, husbands, or lairds. Rachael was glad she was being presented as the fiancée to Duncan and was glad she could observe the king's reaction to Duncan. This was a thrill any historian from her time would have gladly witnessed. 'Where were you' moments she called them. Moments in history that became larger than life moments and you would remember where you were. She remembered the story her mother would tell of what she was doing when news came through that Princess Dianna had died.

Now it was her turn to experience one of those moments. Just very strange that it involved a moment of history nearly two hundred years before she was born. One she would never be able to share in her future. But one she could hold in her heart. Duncan came over and placed his hand in hers.

"Are you ready to meet the king, my dear?"

"No, but let's do it anyway." She gave him a smile and squeezed his hand. They headed to the corridor that led to the meeting room. There was a line but a gentleman who was dancing around, made sure that people were in the right place. The master of ceremonies she assumed.

He came to them and addressed Duncan. "Who are you presenting, sir?"

"My sister, Miss Glenna Murray, The Honourable Miss Delia Farraday and my fiancée Miss Rachael Fielding of Australia." Duncan looked at her with a smile of pure devotion and pride. She could have cried.

"A colonist. How exciting. The king will be delighted, no doubt." The dancing man continued his dance down the line of people behind her.

The line moved slowly and steadily through various anti-rooms leading up to the entrée room where the king waited. This gave Rachael time to view the many ladies and the splendour they wore. Many were overdressed as far as Rachael was concerned. Her simple but elegant dress suited her. She certainly did not want to adorn herself in tassels, abundant feather, turbans, or highland bonnets. Simple was what she was and needed to be today. She did not want to draw attention to herself.

She looked around the palace and saw that it was much the same as she remembered when she had visited it in the future. Except that it had more furniture and paintings in this moment than in the future. It seemed both lived in and homely.

They were about to go through the doors into the room of the king when she could feel Duncan place something around her bare neck. She reached up and felt a single stone on a delicate chain. She looked down and saw a simple yellowish stone.

"It is the stone of the Cairngorms. I want you to wear it as a promise from me to you."

Trust Duncan to give her a gift in a place she could not object. It seemed he also knew her well. She lifted her head and smiled into his waiting gaze.

"You shouldn't have but I thank you with all my heart."

"You are most welcome."

The door into the room where the king waited opened and they went through.

Within moments they were in front of the king.

"Murray, who do you have here that I must make acquaintance?"

The king gave a little grin as he looked at Glenna and Delia in turn. But she shook with fear as his eyes alighted on her and did not move on. She gave a little smile but saw the eyes of a wolf resting on her. All knew he was a philanderer but was shocked to see he was so open about it. Duncan distracted him.

"Your highness. May I introduce my sister, Miss Glenna Murray?" The king reached over and pecked Glenna on the cheek, but his eyes stayed glued to her. This was extremely disconcerting. Duncan grabbed hold of her hand and she looked up into his worried eyes. She tried to give him a reassuring smile.

He then introduced, "The honourable Miss Delia Farraday." The king greeted her also with a kiss on the cheek and said, "It is a pleasure to see you again, Miss Farraday." This was out of sequence, but she was sure that Duncan had done it deliberately so that she would be introduced last, and that he could get her away from here quickly.

Now came the moment of truth. "And who, Murray, is this beauty? I dare say she is not Scottish."

Duncan smiled but hung on to her hand almost to prevent her from running. At this moment, meeting the lecherous king, because that is the way she perceived him, was the last thing she wanted to do. But Duncan prevented her escape.

"This sir, is my fiancée, Miss Rachael Fielding." There was a clear emphasis on the 'my'. Duncan gently pulled her toward the king. She turned her head at the last second so that the king planted a big sloppy kiss on her cheek. He had been aiming for her mouth.

"A true beauty. You are a lucky man."

Duncan bowed and she curtsied, and they went on their way. Rachael was shaking. He had spoken to none of the other Scottish ladies who were in front of her, nor those who came up behind. He greeted Delia who he knew from the English Court. All the gazes of the Scottish ladies who were in the room were glued on her. They exited the room slowly and went back into the anti-room they had previously been in. As the doors closed, Rachael voiced her distaste in the only way she knew how.

"Oh yuck. What a pervert."

A shudder went up and down her body and she shook herself to remove the feeling. She looked at Duncan, Glenna, and Delia in turn. All looked stunned at her comment.

"Well, he is a big fat pervert."

They all burst into laughter. Duncan held her to his chest and whispered, "Good response." She was not sure what he meant but was sure he was pleased she disliked the king with a passion. No more 'where were you' days for her if they were going to be like this one. This was one part of the history she would have been happy to forgo.

He had to admit as he hugged her to his chest, that he was delighted with her response. Someone had informed the king about his fiancée and he wanted to somehow distract him from her. But every time they met, he continued to ask questions about how he got to 'know the lovely lady he was hearing so much about.' To the king's annoyance Duncan did little to encourage him. It made him ask more questions about Rachael's sudden arrival and if she had links with the king. Her obvious fear of meeting him added to his dismay. But she had responded to the king with utter disdain. And that was no play acting. She hated him.

Now in the carriage ride home he held her close to him pleased that meeting the king had seemed somewhat of a disaster for her. All continued to describe the king in not so pleasant terms. She had no connection to him.

"I am very annoyed Duncan that you did not tell me he was so fat. I nearly laughed in his face. But watching him, dare I say, lust after Rachael, made my stomach turn inside out." Glenna pulled a face and he had to agree that the experience made all of them cringe.

"The feeling is mutual." Rachael too pulled a face.

"Well, it is done. I dare say he will head back to Dalkeith and we need not worry about him for a time. Society will meet but quite frankly I have had enough of it for a while."

He watched Rachael close her eyes to try to bring back to her memory some further piece of history.

"Thursday is the king's review, is it not?" She asked, hoping someone would answer.

Duncan spoke first. "Yes, it is. Do you wish to go?"

"Oh yes, lets. It should be a most grand affair. I hear that Scott has gone to great lengths to show off our 'Scottish roots' and all the manpower that we have at our disposal." Glenna said.

Rachael laughed. "The poor man. But he will be in luck this time as the sun will shine and you could say it will be almost hot. I have no desire to be there, but you go. I think I have had my fill with royalty for the time being."

"One viewing and you are giving up, my dear." He was teasing her of course.

"Yep. I've had it. That man…yuck."

This time it was Delia who began to laugh.

"I love it." She said. "I can't wait to tell my father. 'Yuck'."

And she started laughing again. This time all the young ladies laughed, and he was happy to join in.

FEAR

W *ednesday 21ˢᵗ August 1822*

The day was a welcomed quiet day. Duncan and Hamish had business to attend to so left early in the morning. Rachael spent most of the day reading various books from the shelves in the study. She also went and sat by the windows watching the passing traffic of people and carriages. She took notes in a small book she had obtained on one of their shopping trips. She jotted down the colours of clothing. Descriptions of people and of the many servants who went in and out the houses, performing the duties that were required.

She spent some of that time thinking of possible story lines for books she might write. Would she continue to write if she was now staying in the past? Was it something that she could still enjoy doing even if she never ever published another book? Using a pencil and not relying on electronics was a delight that she had not expected. Being alone, taking notes and loving the peace and quiet helped to relax her.

The men returned for luncheon and Duncan asked Rachael to come out for a stroll. After all the weather was fine.

"I guess that I just remember the events because of the weather." She was trying to explain to Duncan that the weather in a story made a big difference to her. "Where I come from…"

"I know, the sun is always shining. I cannot imagine a country like that. Scotland can experience all conditions in one day cold warm, never hot, raining, and cloudy."

"I know summer, winter, autumn and spring all in one."

"Exactly."

"Duncan, was there something particular that you wanted to talk to me about? The weather can be fun, but it seems a strange thing to chat about even for me. And you seem somewhat distracted."

"I did want to discuss something a little more serious. It is the king. I just want to warn you to keep away from him at the ball on Thursday evening. The Peer Ball will be on after his sunny day of reviewing the guards and the parade as you have said."

"Why would I need to be anywhere near him?" Duncan looked at her with concern in his gaze. But she also noticed he wouldn't keep his eyes on her as he usually did. He was distracted, she could tell.

"I believe, and you know his reputation, he has his eyes set on you as his next conquest. He is openly discussing it." He had stopped walking and was looking intently at her now. She turned to face him.

"Bully for him. I have no desire to be anywhere near him, let alone have an affair with him." Her body shivered and it was not cold. "What on earth makes you think that I would do that especially with him?" She screwed up her face. "This is giving me a very bad taste in my mouth. Don't you trust me?"

"I trust you, but I don't trust him."

"I am no little snivelling wimp of a girl. I do not like him so there will be nothing to worry your pretty little head about." She turned to head to the house. Then she turned back toward him. "I do not like him. Get it. You make me so angry." She turned and started toward the house again. Duncan grabbed her arm.

"Please understand that it is him I am concerned about. What he could do to you if you refuse him."

She turned to face him again. She took a few deep breaths. Her anger was subsiding. He was right. This was a man with a great deal of power who could make her and Duncan's life miserable.

"I do not want to be near him. There is nothing between us." She lowered her head feeling deflated. "Well, it's simple, you, Alasdair and Hamish had better keep your eyes on me and never leave me alone. That way he won't get near me, will he?"

"We will, I promise you. You are pre-warned so now you can prevent his getting near you also. I am sorry if you think I do not trust you. It is him I do not trust. I fear he will hurt you."

"I understand that you want me to be armed against his advances. I will be now. I'm sorry for my reaction. I just…"

They spent a few moments looking into each other eyes, and she could see the love had returned. Then Duncan offered his arm and they headed back to Charlotte Square.

The evening was occupied with some business dinner guests. It was rather interesting to watch but Rachael was exhausted and excused herself early to retire to bed. She waited up for a while, but Duncan did not come. She laid down on the bed to continue her vigil but fell asleep.

THE BALL

Thursday 22*nd* August 1822

Rachael stretched and then sat up, surprised that she was in her own bed. She had slept the night through, and Duncan had not disturbed her. She got up and went to open the curtains. She paused. Was her anger from yesterday an issue?

Of course not. He just wanted me to rest. After all the Peer Ball is tonight.

She went back and got into bed and lay there for a few minutes. The maid soon entered with her tea. She placed it on the table and then headed to the door to leave the room.

"Grace, what time is it?"

"Ten o'clock miss. The morning is nearly gone."

Rachael sat bolt upright. "Why didn't you wake me earlier?"

"The laird, miss, insisted that you sleep till ten. That is why I have come in now and not earlier."

"Oh. Very well. Where is the laird?"

"He had an errand to run but has left you a note, miss." She put her hand in her apron pocket and pulled out a handwritten and sealed note for her eyes only. She placed it on the table next to her tea. "I almost forgot. Sorry miss."

Rachael scrabbled out of bed and Grace went over to the chair and picked up her dressing gown which she held up to allow her to put it on.

Grace then left the room. The servants know when to leave a room and allow private moments. She walked over to the table and sat down in the chair next to it. She picked up the letter and opened the seal.

My dearest Rachael,

I do apologise that I did not take you to my room last evening. I came to you, but you were fast sleep. I did not have the heart to disturb you. Especially as I had an early start again this morning. I have again been summoned by the king for some 'private words'. I do not know what they are about. You were right again. If you look outside you will see the sun shining. Will it last?

I will be home in time to change and escort you and Glenna to the ball. Have a restful day. Tonight, will be a busy one.

Always yours

Duncan

She held the note to her heart. Even if all goes wrong, she will have this piece of him to remember him always. She shook her head. What was she thinking? They had already decided to marry, and she had decided to stay here. She folded the note and placed it in her lap. She poured a cup of tea and looked out the window. Yes, the sun was shining. Just as she remembered from her readings. Cup in hand, she sipped her tea.

Glenna, still in her dressing gown walked into the room. She had her cup in hand and sat down in the chair opposite Rachael. She took Duncan's word and planned to have Glenna be part of the watch and protect party.

"You were allowed to sleep in, too. You have a generous brother."

"I'm glad of it." Glenna sighed. "The Peer Ball tonight will be a bit of a squash. The assembly hall is large but with all the guests in from all over Scotland, I am imagining a squeeze. The Peer Ball is the highlight of the calendar." She sat back in her chair and sighed. "I see Duncan let you sleep in also. Concern is written on your face, my friend. Why?"

"Clairvoyant as always. Duncan spoke to me when we were on our walk yesterday. He thinks that the king wants to make moves on me." Glenna looked at her with confusion on her face. "Sorry, he wants me to be his next dalliance."

"Oh, yuck. I love that word. It describes the king perfectly."

She paused, looking at her with eyes that indicated sadness.

"I have no intention of being his conquest, I can tell you. The thought gives me goose bumps." She rubbed her arms in anticipation of the event.

"I know. But this puts you and Duncan in a terrible place. What can I do to help?"

"Well, Duncan thinks that is simple enough. We must keep directing me away from the king and the king away from me. Sounds simple, doesn't it?" Even hearing her own voice, she did not seem convinced.

"We can only try and do what we can. I will gladly help. No doubt Duncan will have Hamish and Alasdair helping to stop the king 'making moves' on you, as you say. Come let us dress and go down for breakfast. I plan to do very little till tonight."

The ride to the assembly halls was not far but Duncan had no intention of them walking in. He also wanted a vehicle that he could use to take Rachael away quickly if the king got too close for his liking. That however was a mistake. They had taken to the carriage at 7.45pm but joined a line at the end of Charlotte square. It took nearly an hour to get to the main door. The carriages were so many, and the drivers so upset, that Duncan almost decided to walk. One hundred yards from the entry he did that and told his coachman not to wait but go straight home. Thus Alasdair, Duncan, Glenna, and Rachael descended from the carriage and walked the rest of the way. There were just as many people on the pavement as carriages and horses on the street, but they soon made it to the foyer.

Duncan noted the squash and took the young ladies into the main ballroom and found a sofa on which to sit them. He returned momentarily with a glass of punch for each of them and news that the king had not yet arrived.

He also noted that the ballroom had been redecorated with fine yellow and blue calico, looking like silk. Flowers were draped around columns and sofas and chairs scattered in every available corner. He viewed the building, to determine ways in and out and places to conceal Rachael once the king arrived. This was no simple assembly. For him it was like preparing for a battle and in a way it was. He must protect Rachael from the king at all costs. He would never forgive himself if she were cornered by him.

Thus, the evening moved on with him, Hamish, Alasdair, and Glenna making sure that nothing could hurt his Rachael.

The ball was crowded and stuffy. She sat there alone and under no illusion that she was enjoying herself. She was not. Under normal circumstances, she would have been lapping up all around her. She was enjoying seeing the beautiful clothes but just waiting for that announcement that the king had arrived, had her frozen to the seat. They had been waiting for some time and the king had not yet made his appearance. Perhaps he would stand them up? After all he had been out all day.

Duncan had refused to say what the king had wanted to see him about that morning. She was also concerned that he was watching everything going on around him as if he were looking for something. He seemed worried and that disturbed her. She knew that he would keep her away from the king. Perhaps that was all that disturbed him.

She asked him to seat her in the corner near a room divider. Surely the king could not reach her there. It was out of the way and far from the entrance to the assembly. Alasdair took Glenna out for a dance. Hamish excused himself but she could still see him and he her. Duncan came up to her.

"I will fetch you a drink, my love. Do not move from here. I will return shortly." Then he was gone.

She was happy to be sitting in a corner behind a column. A room divider was at her back. Almost everyone else was on the dance floor. Behind the room divider a window was open, and a gentle fresh breeze was wafting in around her and the divider. But that was not all. Voices were drifting in too. They were loud enough for her to hear but not for the crowd on the dance floor. She listened with interest.

"I tell you he won't come." The voice sounded scared almost fearful. It continued "What are we to do? It depends on this place and time."

Another voice, deeper and more assured, answered. "Do not lose your nerve. He will be here. Scott will see to that. This is his final ball. And our last chance."

"But what if...."

"Enough. The king will die tonight."

Rachael didn't move and placed her hand over her mouth to stop her mini scream. The deeper Scottish voice continued.

"There will be no more George."

"But Bevan…"

"Quiet. Do not call me by my name. Come, we will wait at the appointed place."

Rachael sat stock still. Not only did she not want to move but her mind was going over all her history. No one made an attempt on the king's life. She had no memory of that at all. What the hell was she going to do?

"Rachael, here is a drink…Whatever is the matter?" Duncan placed the drinks on the table next to her chair and dropped to his knee in front of her. He took her cold and shaking hands into his.

"Rachael?"

She drew her attention to Duncan kneeling in front of her. "The king…" was all she could get out.

"I'm sure he will be here soon. Do you wish to see him again so soon?" She did not appreciate that he was teasing her.

"No. Duncan get the family and take us where it is quiet. I must talk to you all."

He rose slowly. "Very well, but what is this about?"

"Hurry, please." She stood and swayed a little. He took her by the arm and escorted her toward the balcony.

"No, not out there." She knew she was scaring him with her raised voice and her insistence. Alasdair arrived with Delia on his arm.

"Take Rachael to the cloak room. I'll get Glenna."

"She is dancing with Hamish. Are we leaving?"

"No. Just go. I will meet you there."

Everyone moved and Rachael was sure she was going to be sick, as the stuffy room drew in around her again. Within minutes they were all in the cloak room. She was shaking and not sure now that she had not dreamt it all.

"Rachael, tell me what is troubling you."

She blurted out what she had heard and the name she had

heard, Bevan. Did Duncan know anyone by that name? He stared at her. The name meant something to him. He became serious.

"What is it that you want me to do?" he asked.

"Duncan, we have to stop the king. History does not want him to die. There is no record of this attempt on his life. We have to make sure that it doesn't happen."

"How do you know what history wants?"

"Duncan please..." Rachael began to cry but his face remained still, unmoved.

"Duncan? We have to keep the king away." That was Glenna. Glenna put her arms around her waist to help her stand.

"I want nothing to do with this. If the king dies, who am I to stop it?" The old Duncan was in front of her.

Why had he changed?

The tears were streaming down her face. This was not the man she had grown to love. It was the Duncan she had first met. The suspicious one. The one who did not trust her. The one she hated. His face had no softness. It was hard and determined.

Could he have something to do with the plot? Surely not. If he changed history, it would be all her fault. What the hell was going on?

The man she knew would never kill anyone. But did she know the man in front of her? Obviously not. She continued to weep.

"Duncan?" But she fell on the floor in a heap.

"Take her back to the townhouse. Get her gear and Glenna's and escort them back to Castle Buin. Do not stop but for food. I want her under lock and key. Do you understand me?"

"Of course, I do. Glad to see that you have come to your senses. Glenna help me get her to a cab."

Rachael continued to cry. Her heart was broken. She stood with Glenna but could feel the strong arm of Alasdair holding her and preventing her falling again.

Outside at last, she fell into the carriage and Glenna pulled her up onto the seat next to her.

"Do not distress yourself so, Rachael. Duncan must have his reasons for wanting us out of Edinburgh. All will be well."

But Rachael had just lost the world she had so wanted. A world that was Duncan. But he had betrayed her. He had deserted her when she had needed him most.

She turned to see the failing lights of the city she loved. The blackness soon surrounded her. Their carriage did not rush. The dark would not allow it. They stopped briefly for food and a change of horses. Sometimes she slept. Sometimes she stared out the window. Sometimes she cried, as Glenna held her in her arms. Sometimes she stared at Alasdair whose smirk promised a big argument when they reached the castle. The bastard had been pretending all along. Pretending to believe in her. She hated these brothers and her heart was broken.

As the hours passed, she sometimes hoped they would never get there, to Castle Buin. The rain had started again. Perhaps it was in time with her heart? She cried and the sky cried too. But she continued this journey and knew that she would soon be making her way to the fairy hill and home. Away from the wonderful dream that had turned into a nightmare. Back to her own time without Duncan.

"Murray, I must thank you for saving my life. You must be honoured in some way. How can I truly thank you for saving your king?"

Duncan bowed to the king. Yes, his king. He owed that to Rachael. She had turned his world on its head. He could not allow the king to die. He had heard rumours of some scots who wished to rid themselves of the king but did not believe them. When Rachael had overheard the plotters and had seen her fear, he had lost his temper. Not at her but at Bevan and his crew. Just as he wouldn't allow the king to die he was not going to leave her to be unprotected. Getting her out of Edinburgh was the most important thing. He knew that Bevan Ramsey would not stop if he heard that Rachael had overheard his plot. He would want both her and the king dead.

Once he knew she was safely away he gathered loyal Scots and even Scott himself and told them what she had overheard. He did not doubt her for a moment, but he wanted her to go. To be safe. Away from Bevan, the king and danger.

"Your highness. Bevan has been taken to the castle and we will deal with him. But I would rather that this attempt on your person not be known, and my part in preventing it. There may be other plotters and we want them to know that you are safe and sound. For me that is all the reward I need."

"You have taken much on yourself, Murray. Thank that lovely woman of yours. You, sir, are a very lucky man."

"Yes sire. I believe I am."

"I will not forget what you have done for me this day."

The king then made his entrance at the ball. He mingled with the guests, Duncan, and Scott never far from his side. The king stayed just slightly over an hour. He then departed to Dalkeith. No knowledge of the attempt on his life was revealed by those who knew. Duncan was just happy that Scotland would not be blamed, had the king been killed. And that its reputation displayed no plot against his highness. Scotland was safe, Rachael was safe and that was all that mattered.

BACK TO CASTLE BUIN

S*aturday 24th August 1822*

Duncan came into the house at Charlotte Square. And not for the first time he wished his love were here. But she was safe. She should be arriving at the castle today if Alasdair had kept his promise. Bevan Ramsey was in the castle dungeon. By agreement with the king he was to be sent into exile on a rock off the west coast of Scotland to spend the rest of his days. Hamish would make sure that he sent news when his sentence was carried out. And he had kept his word that what had taken place would not be generally known.

He went and sat in the day room and waited for his tea. So much had happened. So much change. The biggest being his attitude to the king. But not the biggest. Falling in love with Rachael was definitely the biggest change. Hamish entered the room.

"Well brother, you can be proud of yourself. I am sure that father and mother would be." He sat down on the sofa next to his brother. The servants followed in and placed a table and tea in front of the two men.

"I would imagine so." He waited for the servants to leave and then continued. "Would father really have honoured the king? But more so, Hamish, I really do not want to do this job. Be the laird." Finally, he voiced his concern to his brother. Rachael had encouraged him to do so. And here he was doing it. He had assumed that he would have kept this from everyone for the rest of his life. And just carried on.

"I know. I think that I have always known. What are you going to do about it?"

He stared at Hamish. "You already knew? Seems everyone else knows me better than I know myself." He sat looking into his teacup for a moment. "I want to go to the future with Rachael. Perhaps I could become a teacher. A teacher of history."

"Do you think that you could be happy?"

"If I am with Rachael, yes I think I could."

"Then do it."

"What of the Lairdship and all that we have planned for the clan's future?"

"Alasdair will make a good laird. You already know that. Glenna will keep him on the straight and narrow till he finds a wife. Perhaps Delia will finally catch his eye. She has been wanting him long enough. And we will go ahead with the suggestions that Rachael made. She spoke the truth and only wants the best for the clan. Good woman."

"Just like that, you want me to leave?" He stood and began to pace the room. "You believe all that Rachael has said about the future? That I would never see my family again if I believe all that she has said?"

"Brother, you love Rachael with all your heart. I can see that. I think we all can see that. You need to be with her. She is not safe if the king really wants her. He will pester you till he gets what he wants. So, go. Rachael will, deep down only want to be where you are. Go to her future. You know that what she has said is the truth. See what the future will do for you. For the both of you."

"Yes, she is telling the truth. I know that. I appreciate what you are saying but I will need to check with Alasdair and Glenna. Tis a big move and one I might not be able to come back from. We need to be sure. I need to be sure."

"Then leave for Castle Buin today. Discuss it with everyone and then make your decision. In the long run, you will be better for it. I will agree with whatever you decide. You kin?"

He came back to the sofa and sat down. He slapped his brother on the back in a friendly gesture.

"I will. Thank you. Thank you for telling me what you think. Thank you for believing in us."

"Tis not hard brother. Remember the stories Father shared? Remember Mother and the special love they shared? You also are being given a special gift. Honour it. There is more to the fae…"

Duncan picked up his cup and drained the contents. He filled the cup again and smiled at his brother. He would miss his counsel. He was sure that Hamish was the only sensible one in the family. Much like his father.

"We should be back at the castle in a few hours. Now that the sun has risen high, we should not experience any delays. The rain appears to have stopped."

Rachael heard his voice but ignored it. She really didn't care what he said. Her world had ended. She knew that in a few hours she would be home. In Scotland of 2018. Without Duncan. Her heart ached. She was sure that any moment it would explode out of her chest and lay on the ground with its last beats pulsing on the floor.

"Rachael, did you hear me?" She lifted her lead weighted head to look at Alasdair. She said nothing.

He touched her leg and she jumped. Scowling at him. She then looked at Glenna on the seat opposite. She was fast asleep.

"You know that I wanted you when you first came?" He leant towards her and his breath thick with whisky, penetrated her senses.

"Take your hand off my leg." She snarled. She moved his hand. "Do not touch me again."

"Ah, you still do have some fight left. When I have you back at the castle, I will take you. You need to fulfil my needs now."

She placed her hand on his chest and pushed him away. "Like hell I will. What do you take me for? Duncan might not love me anymore, but I still love him. I would not be with you if I were dead."

"I could arrange that if you like." His look was that of a wounded animal. If she pushed him too hard, he might just attack. She placed her hands in her lap.

"Alasdair, you are a liar. How could you do that to me, let alone your brother? And what of Delia? I was stupid to think that you were a gentleman. You're a drunk. A drunken fool."

"My brother hates you." His tortured expression reminded her of the face of her ex when she told him to get out. Now she hated Alasdair as much as she did Josh. She could so use him now as her new villain. Josh couldn't even be this bad.

"I don't believe it. He loved me once."

"And Delia is nothing to me."

"Pity, she could have been good for you. You are drunk and stupid. But right now, I hate you to the inner most part of my being. Brother or not, I would not lay with you for all the money in the world. I despise you."

He lifted his hand and struck her on the face. Tears filled her eyes, but she did not cry out. She turned to look out of the window and wrapped her travelling coat closer around her. The tears toppled from her eyes. He was drunk. He had been drinking solidly for the two days since they left Edinburgh. He was a wasted man. She would never respect him again.

Go to hell, bastard.

"Take it carefully. You should make Perth before you need a change of horse. There is no need to rush."

"Thank you, Hamish, for your clear counsel. I will miss you. Be assured of that."

"I want you to be a happy man. Find your happiness with Rachael. Enjoy the love that our father and mother once shared. Save it for your whole life. And if you ever have a son, perhaps you can name him after me. Enjoy your future."

They laughed and hugged each other. Soon Duncan was on his black stallion and heading home.

The carriage pulled up in the carriageway in front of the castle. Servants came pouring out of the main doors to collect luggage and help their master and mistresses from the coach. Great care and attention was shown to her. Seems they had not heard that their laird had disowned her. She stretched and gently adjusted her posture. She was stiff and sore.

"I will be sure that your belongings are taken to Duncan's room." Glenna gave her a hug.

"That would not be wise. He has deserted me. He would not like me in his room for any reason."

Glenna sighed. "Well, that is where you are going. As far as I am concerned you are for Duncan. I heard Alasdair. He needs to remember his place. Take Duncan's room and lock the doors. Do you hear me? Do not go near Alasdair."

"Playing possum, were you? I will take the room but not for long. Glenna, I need to return to my time. I can't stay here. Duncan does not love me; Alasdair hates me, and the king probably will hunt me down."

"I do not agree with your conclusions but perhaps for now you can just rest and get some sleep. Let us wait till Duncan gets back."

"Very well." But a plot was hatching in her head. A plot to get back to the time she was from and not stay in the time that she wanted to be in. Duncan did not love her. That was all she could think of.

She followed the servants up the steps. Alasdair called out to her.

"Rachael, I must speak with you."

"Go to hell." She yelled and continued into the castle. She watched as the servants could not look her in the face as they had before. They were embarrassed that their 'new lady' spoke so to their master. She would never be forgiven.

"What did you think she would say after the way you have treated her?"

"You heard me." It was an admission not a question. Glenna nodded her head.

Glenna slapped him on the chest. "The poor thing thinks that Duncan does not love her anymore. She is devastated and you tried to take advantage of her. You should be ashamed of yourself. You are her brother. We have to convince her that Duncan still loves her."

Alasdair's head was lowered, and Glenna could see his embarrassment clearly.

"But he doesn't. He knows now that she is a plant by the king."

"Hogwash. You have to be one of the most confused of my brother. Even Duncan did not give me this much pain. I guess you cannot see that Delia, for some stupid reason, is in love with you either?"

"No, I can't. She is? Are you sure?"

"Men." She turned and walked away.

Rachael found that her other items including her future clothes had been placed in the master's room. First thing was to bathe as she had two days of travelling grime and wanted to feel whole again. She ordered a bath. Alasdair knocked on her door twice and she in no uncertain terms told him to bugger off.

Eventually he gave up. Glenna came to see her after her bath. Rachael was in a robe. A robe Duncan had ordered in the city and had sent home. Before he had changed his mind.

"I wish you would see that he still loves you."

"Glenna, I will miss you more than you will know."

"Miss me, what are you saying? You are not going anywhere."

"But there is nothing for it. I can't stay. Duncan does not love me."

"Ridiculous. Alasdair told you lies because he was drunk. Duncan has not deserted you."

"Then what am I doing here? Tell me that. If he loved me, he would be here. I have no choice, I have to leave. If I stay, he will humiliate me again and turn from me. I could not face that rejection"

"And where, sister, would you go?"

It was strange that Glenna would even ask such a question. After all there was only one other place for her.

"Home, Glenna. Back to the future. I should never have come here. I wish I had never dreamt of Duncan."

"You were meant to come here. Do not say that. Promise me you will sleep on it and then we can talk. We do not understand all that has taken place."

Rachael had her finger crossed behind her back and she nodded. She had no intention of staying and being humiliated again.

"I'll have some food sent up and you can stay in here for the night. We will talk later." She walked to the door. "Do not let my brother in."

"You don't need to worry about that. Him, I do not trust. See you in the morning."

Rachael felt dreadful that nodding to her friend was telling her a lie. She was going home tonight. Glenna left her. She got out her jeans and shirt and her coat. She found her bra and panties. She dressed. Now her shoes.

She started to cry remembering Duncan said that he hid them from the servants so they would not see them. She looked around as the tears ran down her face. He was the laird so he would hide them where he would believe them safe. She began to search his room. She went through draws and cupboards. She found things that she knew were meant for her. She gripped the stone around her neck. The one he gave her to remind her of his promise. She slipped it off and placed it on the bed. A bed she would not share with him.

She sat on the floor and cried till all her tears had dried on her cheeks. She must have fallen asleep. The knock on the door woke her. Standing up, she asked who it was.

"It is your supper, madam." She unlocked the door and let the servants in. Alasdair was standing across the corridor.

"May I speak with you?"

"No. Go away." He stood there with a pitiful look upon his face, but she would not relent. "We have nothing to say to each other."

He bowed his head but did not move. "I am sorry."

"I don't care. Get lost."

The servants left and she locked the door again.

She hoped they had not noticed that she had changed into her old clothes. She wanted to get away soon and had no desire for them to follow.

She ate what she could and left the rest. She still had not found her shoes. She had checked every cupboard and box. Then she looked down and realised she was sitting on a chest. She tried to open it, but it was locked.

Great, now what?

She paced back and forth for a minute and then remembered seeing a key in the draw of his table near the fireplace. She went and got it and tried to see if it would open. It did not. But another cupboard draw was locked so she tried to open it with the key she had. And it opened. Inside the draw she found some interesting things.

There was a little wooden toy. A relic from his childhood no doubt. Some rocks. Perhaps he had collected them as a child. A piece of tartan material the size of a handkerchief. A diamond broach that she assumed belonged to his mother. She would never know. Not now. There was also a key. A much bigger key and just the right size for a big travelling chest. She picked it up and walked back to the chest she had been sitting on. Reverently she placed it in the lock. It worked. She opened the lid and knew that some of Duncan's favourite and cherished things would be in here.

Sitting on the top were her sneakers. She took them out but carefully lifted the cloth on what the shoes had been placed upon. She wanted to see what else was inside. She still loved him and wanted to know what he treasured. It was a tartan. And a very old one. There was a sword on top of it and a sporran. They must be significant family heirlooms. There was a necklace also. It was very similar to the one Duncan had given her. She looked at the bed and saw that her necklace was still laying there. She closed the lid and locked it and returned the key to the draw where she found it.

This was too painful. She put her shoes on and then went to the window. It was dark at last. She went to the door and unlocked it, opened the door ever so slightly. Alasdair was still there. She closed the door and locked it again as he muttered something to her that she could not make out.

What the hell was she going to do? She would never get past Alasdair. She sat on the bed for a few minutes and then she jumped up when she remembered that the servants had a back entrance into the bigger rooms. Glenna had one so perhaps Duncan had one too. She searched and found what was meant to be a hidden door. But she could see the wear and hand marks from years of use. She opened it and found narrow stairs leading down. Great, she was out of here at last.

FAIRY HILL

She was almost there. A few more minutes and she would be at the top of the hill. She looked back and around her and was sure no one saw her escape the kitchen. They were all so busy. And she had not heard a sound since she headed for Fairy Hill. She could only assume no one was following her. Now, if she could only get back to her time. What little energy she had, was pushing her along. Could she now save her broken heart from completely crashing? Her time was short before she ended up on the floor again weeping uncontrollably.

Reaching the top of the hill, she went straight to the centre stone and laid down. She was cold. But that was in part due to her emotions. In a few minutes she could calm herself enough to fall asleep. She would wake up in the 21st century alone. But that was better than being stuck in 1822, hated by the man who once loved her more than she could imagine. Or by being pursued by his brother who wanted her dead because she didn't want him. And finally, by a king who was just a straight out dirty old man.

She practiced her meditation skills, not used for some time, and slowed her breathing. The scent of the beautiful grass had lulled her to sleep in the future, so she concentrated on that. It helped her stay calm. And thinking of 2018 and home.

Alasdair slipped silently through the trees. He saw her climb the Fairy Hill. Why on earth was she coming here? Did she know that he was following and wanted to continue the masquerade?

"No, she does not. She wants to go home." Glenna stepped in front of him.

"Where the hell did you come from?" He looked from side to side as if expecting more of her to appear.

"Did you think you were the only one who could step quietly through the forest, brother?"

"So, you thought she would escape, too."

"No actually, she told me she wanted to go home."

"But then why in God's name has she come up here?"

"Oh, Alasdair you cannot be as slow in the head as you are making out to be. She is going home to the future. And once and for all you will see that the fairies do exist, and you need to do some serious soul searching." Her hands were on her hips and she was shaking her head. "Now, do not make a sound and I will show you. Life has a lot to offer you if you dare to believe."

He stood looking at her, shocked and somewhat bewildered. But he quietly followed her to a nest of trees at the top of the hill. Before they reached the top, she turned and made one more comment.

"Do not make a sound or you will regret it."

Her tone made it clear he had better listen to what she said. When did his sister become so bossy?

They made it to the top and he could see Rachael laying on her back on the rock in the centre of the hill. She did not move. Then she turned onto her side and drew her legs up to her chest. He could hear her crying. It sounded like a wounded animal preparing to die. After a few minutes, the crying ceased.

Alasdair looked at his sister who held her finger to her lips to indicate quiet. After a few more minutes he noticed a faint glow of cold blue green light coming from Rachael's still figure. He again looked at his sister who again gave the sign for quiet.

The light grew in intensity. He could not take his eyes off the spot. He was sure he had not even blinked. Suddenly Rachael was gone.

"What the…Where is she?"

"I think you can say, 'when' is she? She has returned to 2018."

"You mean to say…"

"Yes, brother, she was telling the truth, from the very beginning. You have so much to learn."

"And how the hell do you know?" She turned and smiled at him and then began to descend the hill. He looked again where Rachael had been. He walked to the rock that she had been lying on and felt the stone. It was still warm from where she had been laying.

He caught up with his sister and really did not know what to say at first. If he had not seen it with his own eyes, he would not have believed it.

"You were given a special gift. A chance to see what the fae are capable of achieving."

He looked at her. How did she always know what he was thinking? How on earth was he going to explain this to Duncan?

"It is time for you to accept that our family has close links with the fae." He shook his head and all the stories he had been told as a child came flooding into his mind.

"You are telling me that our family have fae blood?"

"Yes."

He looked at his sister as she stopped walking to look at him.

"You have fae blood?" he asked.

"Yes. You are beginning to understand. It is not just an interest that I have held. Father revealed to me when I was twelve that I took after my mother in more than a few ways."

"Mother was fae?"

"Yes."

He sat down on the grass where he had been standing. He did not care that the grass was damp. Nothing could have prepared him for the revelations he had just heard. She sat down in front of him.

"Duncan?" he said. "Did he know?"

"He was told by our father, but he did not want to believe it. At least not until Rachael came."

"What about us? We brothers? Are we infected?"

"It is not a disease or an illness, brother, but no. It comes only in the female line in mixed marriages. Yes, father knew mother was fae. But she became a mortal losing some of her powers so that she could be with him and eventually us."

"But she died."

"She became mortal and all of what that means."

His head was hurting but he knew all he was hearing and what he had seen was true. He looked at his sister with a newfound respect. She was not a child. She was special and had every right to turn down his friends as potential mates.

"Thank you." She smiled.

"You are welcome. But I wish you would stop reading my mind." He smiled. "Now, what do we do to get Duncan and Rachael back together? I have been such a fool."

"Yes, you have. Duncan is riding home already. He will be here at luncheon the day after tomorrow."

"How do you know...Forget it."

"We need to have certain things in place. Let us get back to the house and start to prepare." She stood and offered her hand to him.

He got up and then took her hand. He bowed and kissed her fingers. "Thank you, Glenna, for being so patient with me."

"I expect a lot of changes and some apologies." She smiled and put her hand though his offered arm and they returned to the house.

HOME?

S *cotland 2018*

The sun was shining. Had it worked? She sat up and looked around her. Yes, it had. This was the scene she remembered when she had been on the hill all those many weeks ago. She slipped off the rock and went to the edge of the hill. The town looked like the town she remembered. It certainly was not 1822. The black top was shining up at her. It was like a smile had touched her. She turned and headed back to the rock and was surprised to see that her backpack was where she had left it, next to the rock. But she had been gone weeks. Surely there would have been people looking for her.

Mrs Watson from her B&B would have told them that she come up here? This was unnerving. Bending down she opened the bag and pulled out her phone. It was the same day. The day she had left. The battery was still charged, the date was the same.

My God, had she dreamt it all?

All that time in the past and it was but hours since she had departed and then returned. She sat there for a few minutes just looking at her phone. Same day. Could it be the same day? All she had experienced. No, it was not a dream, it was real. She touched her lips and remembered the way Duncan had kissed her. That was no dream. Deep within her she remembered how Duncan felt as he made love to her. She had lost that forever. That pain and anguish she was feeling now was real. Tears again rolled down her cheeks.

Unsure of how long she sat there, she remembered Glenna and the fae. She was a believer. Who would have thought that a logical brain such as hers would ever believe in magic? Real magic. She texted Sam.

'Please come. Urgent. Can't move. Need you.'

She stood and headed down the hill, backpack over her shoulder. Thank goodness the B&B was only a short walk. She got down to the street and saw no traffic. Perhaps the world had come to an end and didn't wait for her? She continued into town and saw that life was still going on. She was so alone. She passed by a black land rover with dark windows. That was all she noticed. She passed it without looking inside and continued down to the main street.

The rest of the walk was a blur.

Two days after Rachael's return to the future, she was still in her room at the B&B. Mrs Watson, the landlady was keeping an eye on her and was bringing her food. And she was glad of it. But Rachael ate little and had not left her room. Mrs Watson had even suggested that she fetch a doctor, but Rachael had refused. She knew what was wrong with her. She had a broken heart.

At about three in the afternoon Rachael got off the bed and sat down in the chair by the window. She thought of another window and another chair with a very different view. In another time and place. She shook her head and looked at the current view.

"What the hell?" There was the black land rover with the tinted windows. That was the same vehicle that had been there yesterday and when she came down the hill. A cold shiver ran down her spine.

Who the hell was watching her?

She was being watched. She kept her eye on the rover as a knock was heard at her door.

"Come in, Mrs Watson."

"Will I do?" It was Sam. Her friend had come. "You look like hell. What has happened?"

Rachael jumped up and threw her arms around her friend, tears again filling her eyes.

"What on earth has happened, Rach? I have never seen you like this. Even when…forget that, what has happened?"

For the next few hours Rachael told her friend what had happened, down to the minutest detail. The clothing, the feelings, the love. All of it. Sam would know not to interrupt her. Rachael had to unburden herself. At last she stopped, and Sam took the moment to put a few words together.

"My dear friend. I really don't know what to say. Fairies and time travel. But I can see this is true. That it is no dream. I have never seen you so desperate. But what the heck are we going to do? Have you thought of going back?"

"A hundred times. But I can't risk my heart again. If I go back and Duncan rejects me, I think I would die." She hugged herself knowing that her words were true.

"I would like to say that you can't die from a broken heart but in your case, I think it could happen. I wish there was something I could do. Bloody men. I have to ask, have you seen any sign of Josh?"

"Why?"

"He was bugging me a few days ago about where you were. I didn't know till just after you rang, from your hill, that one of the staff told him where you were and then he took off. I looked for him, but his mates said he went to Scotland. When I got your text, I went straight to Sydney and flew directly to Glasgow and hired a car. Then, well, here I am."

"That's weird. Before you came in, I had noticed there has been a black land rover parked outside since I got back."

"That can't be right. Because I know that Josh was less than a day ahead of me. He could only have gotten here last night at the earliest."

Rachael got up and went to the window. "Well, that land rover is still there. I haven't seen anyone get in or out of it. I just know that they are watching me."

Sam came to the window and looked out. "Maybe we should go for a walk and see what happens. Or we could call the police?"

"Let me have a shower and dress. I'm a little hungry now. We could go downtown and have dinner?"

Rachael was feeling better than she had for the first time in days. Having her friend Sam helped her come to terms with the fact that her life was never going to be the same again. She missed Duncan and Glenna and wanted to be with both of them again. Stepping out of the B&B she saw that the rover was still there. She looked at Sam.

"It could be my imagination?"

"It could but let's not take the risk. Let's just head for town and get something to eat. And stay on the footpath." She placed her arm in hers and locked together they headed down the road.

The air was fresh, and Rachael took a couple of deep breaths of the Scottish air that she loved. One small tear slipped down her cheek. She wiped it away. Suddenly hands were over her eyes.

"Surprise."

Rachael pulled away and turned around. "What the bloody hell are you doing here, Josh?"

"Surprising you, babe. Showing you that I will travel the world to find you."

"You mean find my money." She had her hands on her hips. "I don't want you here. Go away."

"Now babe, that's not fair. I came to find you."

"Get lost, drop kick." Sam was not going to allow him to get closer to her. She got in front of Rachael and put her hands on his chest and pushed him away.

Rachael noticed figures getting out of the rover and heading towards them. Would they help? Or were these friends of Josh? Rachael turned and started to run. She wasn't waiting to find out. She needed to get away.

"Rachael, my love," came a deep and wonderful voice. She stopped dead, turned, and could see the figure of a man who looked like Duncan running toward her. That was all she remembered.

NO RACHAEL

1 *822*

My God, he hoped that she was all right.

After coming back to the castle and finding Rachael gone, he raged around the castle looking for her. Finally, he had gone to his room. Would he find her waiting for him? He came into the empty room and walked over to the bed and found his promise necklace sitting on the covers.

"It is my fault, brother." Alasdair stood behind him.

"What have you done?" He was holding on to his emotions. His hands were in fists and the desire to hit something was great. His brother had better explain himself.

Rachael. Where are you?

"I thought you had come to your senses and had me take her back to our castle under watch, so that you could reveal to the king that she had betrayed us all."

Duncan picked up the necklace and examined it. His hand

closed around the stone. "She has returned to the future, her future?"

"Yes, Duncan. I drove her away. I tried to take advantage of her. I was drunk. I am sorry. Nothing happened. She saw to that and called me all the names under the sun. I have never heard such language."

Duncan took a deep breath. "Tell me why I should not kill you?" He turned and looked at his brother.

"Because I have a plan. A plan that will reunite you both in a future that is made for you."

Duncan looked down at his promise necklace and placed it in his left hand. He formed a fist with his right and slammed his fist into Alasdair's face.

Alasdair stumbled and landed on his knees on the floor.

"I deserved that I know. But please listen to what I have to say."

"Does Glenna know what you have done?" He was breathing heavy and wanted to hit Alasdair in the face again. But held himself back.

"Yes. In fact, I now know what magic she has. I finally believe what the family has believed in for centuries. I am so sorry that I have hurt you. I am a fool. It took me so long to see what was plain to you, Hamish, and Glenna. You love Rachael."

"I hurt you brother, and I want to hurt you again."

"He sees the truth now, Duncan. I can vouch for that." Glenna came over to Duncan and put her hand on his back. He had no doubt that she felt the growl emanating from deep within him.

"She is my love. What am I to do?" He turned and sat on the bed. He looked up into his sister's eyes. "I cannot live without her." A tear rolled down his cheek. For the first time since his father had died, he allowed his family to witness his grief. He was angry and lost that Rachael had gone to a future without him. That she did not wait for him.

"You will not live without her if you will listen to our plan.

Please Duncan let me make amends." Alasdair walked over to his brother and for the first time, knelt before him. "You are my laird."

"But I don't want to be your laird or anyone's laird. I only want Rachael."

His sister and brother stood there quietly. They did not say a word. Duncan stood and pulled his brother into his embrace.

"I will not kill yee. I beg your forgiveness regards my threat. I feel lost. Let us go downstairs and sit and eat. You can explain your plan to me."

And for the first time in years he planned to tell his family that he didn't want to be laird. That he only wanted Rachael in the future.

FAMILY

2 *018*

Duncan looked out on the Fairy Hill. He had only just arrived. He slipped off to the side into a small crop of trees. There he waited. He watched as Rachael walked up the hill in the still dark night. She sat on the rock. She was talking to something that she held in her hand. He watched her, wanting to embrace her but knowing that he had just a few hours to wait and perhaps he could hold her in his arms again, forever. Glenna said that the fae had given him a gift. That he could see her before she departed to the past. But that he needed to see her leave and then go and see his future family before Rachael would return.

She placed the item she had been speaking to into her bag. Then she laid down onto the rock. After a few minutes as the sky was lightening, the blue green glow came from the rock and Rachael disappeared. He stood and walked to the rock and touched it.

Closing his eyes, he could feel the warmth from the rock, from Rachael, reaching into his being.

"It will not be long now my love. We will be together."

He made his way down the hill and walked toward the castle and hoped beyond hope that his brother's plan had worked.

———

He could not believe how well the castle looked. Not a ruin but a well-kept building. That boded well. The garden and surrounds looked even better than they had in his past. His past. Even the lake looked familiar. Could it be true that he could remain in the future with his Rachael? He walked up to the door and knocked. This was where the plan could unravel. Had his family maintained their lands? Had they made a stronger future for them all?

A beautiful red-haired young lady who could easily have been his sister answered the door. She looked up at him and smiled. "Uncle Duncan, you have arrived."

"I. My name is Duncan. Duncan Murray."

"We know. We have been expecting you. It is so wonderful to meet you."

"It is? Do you know me?"

"No, but you are known to me. I am your great, great, great, great, great grandniece, I think. I am related directly to Alasdair. My name is Anna. Please come in."

Duncan stepped in through the door. He recognised his home immediately but also saw added things around the foyer that indicated that it was not the home he had. A group of people both men and women were making their way toward him across the black and white tiles from his past.

"Can I introduce you to my, our family? This is my mother, Jocelyn." He shook the hand of another lady who looked like an older version of his sister.

"You too are directly related to my sister Glenna, are you not?"

"No actually, I am related to Alasdair and Molly."

"Who is Molly? Never mind."

A gentleman came forward and put out his hand. "I am Duncan. I am so pleased to meet you. And I will fill you in later with all the lines back to your brother. Now come in and have a bite to eat. We need you to get back to Fairy Hill in a few hours."

He walked with them down the hall into the dining room. It was very different but still had many of the things from his home, including the Mahogany table that his father had bought for his mother. He went over and touched it. It was home.

"We will fill you in on all the family details when you have been reunited with Rachael. A few things that we must tell you now so that you will be prepared for the changes."

"Rachael has filled me in on some of the modern things like cars and the changes to the roads."

"That is good. We will take you to where you can watch for Rachael and the B&B that she is staying in." Said Jocelyn.

"Bed and Breakfast. It is like an inn from your time." He looked to the man who had spoken and saw a slightly older version of himself but with redder hair. "I am Duncan also. I am the laird and a direct descendant of your brother, Alasdair."

"I am very pleased to meet you." The man nodded with a slight frown upon his face. "I had doubted the lady's stories despite the letter from your brother that you would actually show up. I must ask, do you plan to take the lairdship from me? It is yours after all."

Duncan was taken aback by the forward nature of the words that came from the current Duncan. "Can we see first that I will be staying? It really does depend on whether I stay. And you must know that I have no desire to be laird."

"As you never returned to 1822, we assume that you will be staying."

"I need to be sure. Can we discuss this later?"

"Of course." But he had an uneasy feeling that he was not welcome here by this new Duncan. He needed to be careful. The women, the ones who held the magic had welcomed him. That would be enough for now.

He saw her walking slowly down the hill. He could see that she had been weeping. He wanted to get out and hug and kiss her.

"I suggest you wait before revealing yourself to her, Duncan. The shock could be dangerous. She is very upset." He was glad that Jocelyn and Anna were the ones sitting with him in this big black machine they called a land rover.

"I am just glad that she has arrived safely. I want to let her know that I am here, but I will take you at your word that she may have difficulty in seeing me now. We must keep watch on her. I do not want her out of our sight."

So, he watched his love walk back to the B&B, crying the whole way. She went inside and he remained outside in this black monster and waited for her. He did not care how long it took. He was going to wait.

It was the morning of the third day of waiting. He knew that she would be in her room full of distress. While waiting he caught a glimpse of another man who was also watching her. He was disturbed when he had shown up the previous evening. He too kept his distance and waited. Who was he? And why was he waiting for his Rachael? Last night he had returned to the castle to eat and sleep. Others watched. They said that they could ring the castle, whatever that meant, and have him here in a moment if she made any movement. Something about a mobile phone. He took them at their word.

But this man had shown up. They had called him early this morning, but the man had not made a move. He had arrived a few hours ago and was waiting. The morning had passed and still no movement. The mystery man had vanished for a while but had returned after luncheon.

His future relations were looking after him and were convincing him that all would be right. He was finding the time waiting unbearable. Then a woman had arrived. She went to be with Rachael. He was sure of that. She was blond and taller than Rachael. She could be her friend Sam. Rachael had discussed her with him.

Then things moved quickly as the sun slowly was sinking. She came out with Sam. She looked tired and sad. And he wanted to hug her more than anything. The man who was waiting for Rachael came up behind her. Rachael looked angry and scared. He had to go to her. He could not wait any more. She started running and he called to her. He now held his beloved in his arms and did not want to let her go.

"Who the hell do you think you are? Get your hands off my girlfriend."

With Rachael in his arms, he turned and headed back toward the B&B.

"Come back here. Did you hear me? That's my girlfriend."

Duncan stopped and looked down at the silent face of his Rachael. Then he turned and looked at the man whom he despised without knowing why.

"This woman, sir, is my fiancée. I suggest you leave." He turned back to the B&B and continued walking into the house. Mrs Watson, whom he had met the night before held the door open as he came in. He went into the parlour and laid Rachael on the lounge. Sam and his family had followed him in. Unfortunately, so had that man.

"She has no fiancée, mate. She is mine." The man yelled.

"Are you Duncan?" Sam asked.

"Yes, I am. And I assume you are Rachael's friend Samantha?"

"Yes I am. She told you about me?"

"Yes. She missed you a great deal. Has she told you everything? About me as well?"

Sam nodded.

Then the man started again. "Then she would have told you about me?"

"Rachael told me of a man who did not love her but loved her money. I am assuming that is you?"

Josh smiled. "I love her. I travelled all the way from Australia."

"Sir, I travelled through time."

"Yeah right."

Duncan came toward him, but he backed away straight into the chest of the driver of the black machine.

"She does not love you. So, leave." He stood in front of the man and looked down on him. The man frowned and had started to sweat.

"I'm not going anywhere. She has to tell me not you."

"Well, hear this Josh, bugger off." Rachael's voice was clear and determined.

"But love, I spent all this money to come to you?"

"I don't care Josh. Get lost."

Duncan turned to see his Rachael sitting up and pointing to the door.

"But…"

"No buts about it, Josh. For the very last time, get out."

"I believe the lady has asked you to leave." He could see that this Josh was most uncomfortable squashed between him and the driver.

Josh turned, passed the driver, and went toward the door.

"You will regret this, Rachael. I can make your life turn to mud."

Duncan had had enough. He went over to Josh and hit him in the face. Josh crumpled to the floor. He did not move. The driver came and grabbed Josh by his coat and dragged him outside. The front door closed.

"Thank you for that. I was just about to get up and do the same thing." Rachael looked at him and he walked over to kneel in front of her.

"Are you feeling better?"

"Yes. I guess I blacked out from lack of food. I haven't eaten much in the last few days."

"I am sorry, Rachael. I had wanted you at Castle Buin to protect you from the man who wished to kill the king. Alasdair misunderstood what I had wanted him to do. Can you forgive me?" He took her hands into his.

"I thought you had changed your mind about me."

"Most assuredly I had not." He reached up to wipe away the tears running down her cheek.

"You came to find me?"

"I did."

"Why?" Her smile indicated that she was toying with him. But he did not mind. If she wanted reassurance, then he would give it to her in bucket loads.

"I love you. I want to spend the rest of my life with you."

"Here or there?" She was not smiling now.

"Wherever you want to be."

He took her into his arms and held her close. "Wherever you are, my love."

He could hear Sam quietly crying. Rachael held him tightly in her arms as well. He did not want to be anywhere else.

WHAT NOW

2 *018*

They were at the castle in the here and now. In a different room to his laird's room. He was now a guest in his own home. And that made her feel rotten. But she was in bed with him knowing that this is where he wanted to be. They had returned to the castle with all her belongings and with Sam. She wanted to talk but the current Murray clan suggested that everyone had an early night and they would all meet in the morning to discuss things.

It was just after dawn and she was quietly listening to the sounds of the house waking up. There was movement down below. Similar sounds to what she had heard long ago. She listened to the birds singing and to the distant drone of a jet aircraft flying overhead. She smiled and laughed a little, knowing that this was the future and not the past. She was in her lover's arms and that was where she wanted to be. She hugged him closer to her.

"Do you wish to talk with me, my love?"

"Always. Sorry if I woke you. I was just listening to the sounds around us. And that made me chuckle."

"I was listening to you breathe. What do you wish to talk about?" He brought her closer into his embrace.

"I guess why you came to the future. I mean I know you said you wanted to be with me, but you gave up so much?"

"Truly my love, what life would I have if I stayed there? Without you?"

"But you have given away your birthright?"

"No. Well yes as laird, I was happy to give that to Alasdair even after what he had tried to do to you."

"You know about that?" she sat bold upright. "I hate him for what he tried to do. But nothing happened."

"I know nothing happened. He is very sorry and blames himself for your departure. I don't think that he will ever get drunk again. Besides, I think that he did a good job in implementing all your suggestions. The family now own a great deal of land. They run the distillery and the shortbread factory. As well as a good many tourist enterprises. And they have you to thank for that."

She took all that in and smiled. Perhaps she could have this new future that was being offered to her. In the arms of a man she had lost. But who came to the future for her.

"When we sit down with the family, we will work out our future and what we want to be a part of. That is the way that Alasdair and I determined it. The current laird thinks that I want to take my position back. But that is not what I want. I didn't want it then so why would I want it now?"

"What do you want?" She turned over so that she could look into his face.

"Apart from you? I am not sure, but history has meant so much to me. That is what I was concentrating on at Oxford before I had to return to our lands when father died."

"Do you wish to teach, write?"

"I really do not know. Do I stay near the family? I just am not sure. But we have time, plenty of time to consider all of that. What I want to know is if you are happy for me to stay?"

"Of course. I want to be with you, so whatever that takes. And you are correct we do have time to determine that."

"Then for now, let us not think on it but be glad that we are together." He drew her close again and she enjoyed the feel of his lips on hers. They had each other and that was more special than anything else. Making love to him was even better.

They made their way down the stairs to the day room assuming that breakfast was still served there. And it was. Everyone else were there waiting, including Sam, who stood and came over to hug both Rachael and him. She had accepted what Rachael had said without question and he knew that their friendship would carry on despite his arrival. And for that he was glad.

"May I introduce Jocelyn and Duncan, the current laird and his sister?" They stood and indicated to Rachael and him to sit down. Next to Jocelyn was her husband, who was part of the family enterprises. Next to the laird was his wife Dianna, who was also a great believer in the magic.

"Duncan, what is it that we need to do?" He asked the current laird.

"I have the letters and diaries your brother wrote after your departure and he wishes that you decide what you wish to do."

He handed the letters to him and for some moments as their breakfast was being served, he read the words from his dear brother's hands.

"I must say that I am very reluctant to hand my lairdship to you despite your right to it." The current laird lowered his gaze to the breakfast on the plate in front of him.

"Well Duncan, please let me ease your mind regarding that. I did not want to be laird in my time, so I will not be wanting it now. I guess we need to discuss where I fit in to this new family, if you will have me."

"You are more than welcome." Anna smiled at him and his Rachael.

Jocelyn added, "The decisions are yours to make but yes you will always be welcome in the Murray Clan, your clan."

The Laird Duncan stood. "I want to welcome you to the family. Both of you. Now let us eat our breakfast then we will go to the study and reveal all that has happened since your departure in 1822."

He looked around at the Murrays. They were familiar. The traits and appearances of his sister and his brother, parts of his mother and father. This was a unique experience as he was aware. How many of the others had been transported by the fairies could or have experienced such things?

The study was warm and cosy. Many of the old books that had been in Duncan's study remained, but it was a lighter and brighter room. But it still was home. Sam was taking a tour of the lands with some of the other family members. But now the current lady and laird and Duncan and she sat ready to discuss their future.

"As to Alasdair's wishes you are entitled to part of the estate that you had given up. We do not wish to deprive you especially as it was due to you and Rachael that our fortunes developed." The laird sat behind the desk.

Dianna, Duncan, and she sat in the chairs that were in front of the desk.

"We can arrange papers so that you become part of this society. Most of that has already been put in place." Dianna smiled at her husband. "Despite many misgivings I thought it was wise to get the ball rolling."

The current laird smiled at his wife.

"As you are aware the magic is only passed on to the women of the family. Anna has been organizing us all for some time to prepare for your arrival. My wife, though not a Murray by birth, has believed in the magic for some time."

"That my dears, is another story. But we need to be thinking about your future. If you will let me, I will tell you what we have prepared and see if that fits into your thoughts and plans."

Duncan leant forward, "I would be delighted to hear. But rest assured I do not want the lairdship. It is yours by right. I gave it to my brother, and you are his direct descendant. It is true. Alasdair and I had discussed it at length before I left."

"Very well. I am sorry for my concern. I even had a letter from your brother addressed to the laird of 2018, saying that you would not want the title." The laird nodded. "Dianna, please tell them what has been arranged."

"We have organised a new home for you on the estate. It is close to Fairy hill and the town but far enough away so that you can have your privacy. Your brother wished for you to have a home here regardless of the decisions you might make. So that you could always come home if you so desired. It is in yours and Rachael's names."

"That is wonderful. And I am very grateful."

Rachael could see that this arrangement gave him great joy, to still be near the land of his birth.

"I was wondering, if I can do some further study and perhaps teach history."

"Your brother mentioned your love of history to me in the letter he wrote. He was honest from the beginning. I still had my doubts that anything would come of the stories."

Dianna smiled at him and she continued. "We have obtained

information on various courses that you can do, or we can also help you to begin teaching in one of them if you decide to not study but start teaching. There are universities in Edinburgh, Glasgow and Inverness and more places around Scotland." She got up and went to a bookcase and brought back a pile of brochures and paperwork. "I am sure that Rachael will help you become acquainted in this new world."

"I am amazed at what you are prepared to do. I also thought that you might want me to work on the land or in some of the businesses that we now have."

"The family are all involved. So, I would suggest that you look around everything and see if any particular area takes your fancy. I do not wish to displace any family member. That is my only concern."

"Of course. I would not want to do that. My brother and you have thought of so many things. I would want to marry Rachael as soon as can be arranged."

"Your personal papers are being prepared so I anticipate that you will be able to do that as soon as we are able."

"This future that we have now involves a great deal of change for me also."

"Yes, it does, and we have not discussed that in full." Rachael added.

The laird stood and went to the window to look out. "Then I suggest that you and Rachael move into your home. Take time to discuss and look around you. Your house will always be yours regardless of what you finally decide to do. After all, Australia could be calling you also."

"It is somewhat overwhelming, and you are right." Her Duncan lowered his head and seemed to be in deep thought.

"Your friend Sam can stay here at the castle but can spend time with you also. We want to give you the freedom and time to think."

Duncan was still deep in thought. "We are grateful."

"The house is stocked with food etc. but come each evening and have the evening meal with us. We can fill you in on all that has happened. There is much that you will need to be aware of. If that suits you?"

Duncan lifted his head, looking first at the laird and then Dianna. "I am most obliged to your thoughtfulness and kindness. I am truly grateful."

The cottage was the most beautiful building she had ever seen.

"This was a hunting lodge in my time, but it is so different. They have made it better than brand new." Duncan continued to walk around the stone building. And he was right. They had renovated it and added more rooms to the building. The garden was well maintained and around the back vegetables and fruit trees were growing.

"I could enjoy living in something smaller than the castle. Besides, it was always cold in that building." He smiled at Rachael and she laughed out loud. She closed her eyes and could hear the birds singing. Yes, she could learn to love living here. Her simple revelry was disturbed by her love. He came and placed his arms around her.

"I must be dreaming. I imagine that the man I love more than anything else, is here with me and holding me close." She opened her eyes. "Ahhh he is."

"Let's go inside and see what is in store for us."

They opened the oak front door and walked into a very modern building. It was as if she had walked into a great renovation show and was seeing the results of all the hard work.

"This is what would be the lounge room and through there the dining room." She walked past the beautiful furniture, modern and clean.

"The furniture is different. That will take me time to get used to."

"Perhaps there are things in the other rooms that will remind you of home." Slowly they made their way around the house. Bedrooms and guest rooms. There was a study that she assumed was for her so that she could continue to write. It was feminine and light. Very French provincial. There was a laptop on the desk. The window was wide and big and gave a wonderful view of the highlands. To the left was a door. She opened it and called to Duncan.

"You have to see this. You won't believe what they have done for you." She was transfixed as Duncan walked into a replica of his old study. It was smaller but his father's desk, many of the books he had known all his life were placed on the replica shelves. He stood there not making a sound. He just looked around at what the future ladies of his family had made for him. The only difference was the laptop on his desk. She would show him how to use it.

"I wish they were here so that I could hug them. They have created the best of both worlds for you, wouldn't you say?"

Duncan turned and took Rachael into his arms. She placed her head on his chest. She could feel the slight vibration in his chest and realised he was crying.

"Are you okay?"

"More than fine, my love. Missing my family but so very glad that I have you. I am somewhat overwhelmed at what Anna, Dianna and Jocelyn have done for me. I could never have hoped…"

He held her close again.

LETTERS AND A FUTURE

August 1823

My dear brother and Rachael

I know that many years lay between us and so much has happened.

I pray that you are together and happy. As you did not return brother, I would say that our adventure was a success.

Rachael, believe me that I now know and believe in your future. I only wish that I could have told you in person.

It is a year since you left, brother. We put into place, a month after you had gone, that you had died at sea while heading to London. It so happened that a boat sank two days before we announced your death and used that tragedy to cover your disappearance. Of course, the family and some of our close servants know the truth. Our hearts are broken at the thought that we will never see you again, but light at knowing you are happy.

We have put into place some of our plans. The village is now ours and some from the Grant clan have come to us and asked to stay. We have agreed.

Other plans will be started soon.

August 1833

Dearest brother and Rachael

The clan are doing well. I have been married for some time now and have already 4 children. The eldest is Duncan and I hope that every first-born son in our line shall be called Duncan in honour of you.

I have two other sons, Lucas and Jasper and a beautiful red headed daughter called Alvina. Glenna chose the name as she will be carrying the fairy line of course.

My wife believes the fairy stories and always has. Can you guess who I married? Of course, you would know all that information from the diaries that I left you. They will show you we have put into place all the things that you and Rachael dreamed would benefit the clan. And we are very grateful.

Our life is good and the country we love, though not doing as well as we, will prosper. We will see to that.

August 1843

My dear brother and Sister Rachael

Twenty years. It is hard to believe so much time has passed. Time. Yes, time is the master is it not? Victoria is Queen, Rachael. Just as you said. They came to Scotland last year and she said how sincerely she loved the place. She has not bought property yet, but I trust that she will because you, Rachael, told me so.

"We are so lucky to have these words from Alasdair. What a wonderful thing for you to hold."

Duncan closed the diary that he had in his hand. "I miss them, but I can see that we made the right decision. Mainly for me that I do not have to live without you in my life."

Rachael got up from the chair in Duncan's study and came around the desk to her love. "I could not imagine life without you and am so grateful that you gave up so much for me."

"It was no hardship. Living without you would have been the worst choice. And besides, you have given up your job in Australia and the life you had there, for me."

She sat on his lap. Her hand held onto the gem that hung around her neck. Yes, his promise, that he made sure to put around her neck as soon as he could. "You know that is no hardship for me. I love Scotland. I miss Sam but she is thinking that now my new book is out I might need her as a full-time assistant. What do you think?"

He held her close. "It is funny that you should say that. Duncan at the manor wants to hire her to put into order the library and all the historical documents of the clan. Perhaps she can do both?"

At that moment Darnit made his way into the study. He stood in the middle of the floor and stretched then rolled over onto his back. Rachael got up and went to her adored kitty and rubbed his tummy.

"I can hear him purring from here."

"It's so strange that he's become an indoor cat here in Scotland and seems not to miss Australia one little bit."

"That's because he has you and is spoilt rotten."

They both laughed.

"I'll email Sam today and see what she thinks. What about your book? How is it going?"

He got up and came to kneel, rubbing Darnit's tummy.

"I am glad you suggested I write Historical Fiction instead of true history. After all, how could I explain some of the things that I know?"

She leant over and kissed him.

"It's been almost two years since we got back from our big holiday to Australia."

"You're not bored, are you?"

"No." She got up and went over to her sofa and sat down. "Just being nostalgic. Besides, I love the fact that this virus has allowed us to be at home together."

"Why don't you tell me what is really on your mind?"

"Ahh dear husband, you read me too well."

"Come on, out with it. Or would you rather I tell you?"

"Claiming the knowledge of reading minds like the fairies, are you?"

He got up and came to sit next to her. "No, just that I know my wife."

"Surprise me, oh great one." She laughed.

"You are with child."

She gazed into his eyes. He did know her. He leaned over and lifted her chin to close her mouth that she had not noticed was open.

"Are you happy about that?" she lowered her head not wanting to look.

"I said that if and when it happened, I would be delighted and I am. Thrilled actually." She threw her arms around him and kissed him.

"I know this virus is a concern. But it happened. I love you." she cried.

"And I love you." They held each other and Darnit came over and jumped onto the cushion next to her.

"Our future will be assured." He placed his hand on her midriff. "We will need to think of names. What about Alasdair?"

She leant over and kissed him. "Our future will be assured be it an Alasdair or a Glenna."

EPILOGUE

Drake walked over to the edge of Fairy Hill where Alvina stood, looking over the edge to the village of Aberlour.

"They are together and expecting a child. Are you content with the result?"

She placed her hand on his shoulder. "Yes. But it is merely the beginning. Other things will need to take place if we are to retain our lands and our position. But yes, it is a good beginning"

"All seems to be heading in the right direction. What more needs to be done?"

"We need to be sure that Glenna and Molly will be able to achieve their part in the story as well as others. But I am satisfied, as you should be. Here we stand on our hill and it is still ours for now."

"And of Molly?"

"Yes, a unique girl, to be sure."

"We have much to be thankful for."

The blue green light on the Fairy Hill faded and was gone.

ABOUT THE AUTHOR

Joanne loves to write and she loves to travel. She is married to Andrew and lives in Central New South Wales Australia with him and their two cats Arthur and Oscar. (Meet them on Joanne's webpage) She has two grown sons and four beautiful granddaughters. Her imagination loves to take her on various trips but mainly in the area of the regency romance.

She also loves meeting new people so do drop a line to her on:

www.JoanneAustenBrown.com

ACKNOWLEDGEMENT

This is a work of fiction, but it is set in real places at a real point of history. King George the 4th did visit Edinburgh in 1822. I did a large amount of research to fit my characters into the events that occurred during his visit. The list below are the main sources for the information that I used.

I also acknowledge my critique partners who never doubted the story within these pages. Fairies, why not. Sue, Rosemary, Kerry and Winsome. Thank you for your input and encouragement.

To my hubby, Mr Romance, thank you. Your support moves me.

Research

The King's Jaunt – George IV in Scotland, 1822 – John Prebble – Collins – 1988

A Dictionary of Scottish History – Gordon Donaldson and Robert S Morpeth – John Donald Publishers – 1977

A History of Scotland – Neil Oliver – A Phoenix Paperback – 2009

Scottish Folk Tales – Lamond Books – 2010

The Penguin Book of Scottish Folk Tales – Edited by Neil Philip – Penguin Books – 1995

My own visits and photography in both Edinburgh and Aberlour.

COMING SOON

Always Elspeth ~ Book Two in the Always series

Coming in February 2021

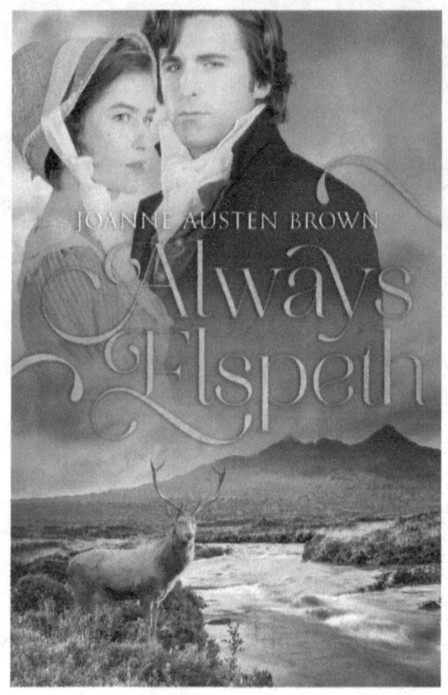

Molly's Laird ~ Book Two in the Come With Me series

Due in October 2021

SAMPLE CHAPTER

Always Louisa ~ Book One: Always Series

1

Summer of 1814

"Do you know why he wants to see me in the library?" They made their way down the hallway. It was abandoned and quiet.

"No, Miss Stapleton."

"Oh, I do wish you would call me Louisa, Chalanor. After all you are Prescott's best friend. And that means we will see a lot more of each other in the coming years. I'm sure you would not want me to call you Farraday, the Viscount Lightford?" Louisa's stomach gave a jolt. Surely, she wasn't attracted to him? He was just Chalanor. She caught her breath and tried to recapture her thoughts. After all she had just become engaged to Prescott. And she loved him. Didn't she?

They continued down the corridor in quiet, the precise tapping of his boots the only noise she could distinguish. When they reached the door Chalanor stopped and turned to look at her. His stern icy blue eyes pierced her own and she shivered.

"Prescott is a lucky man to have won your heart. I hope he realises that."

"That is very nice of you to say, Chalanor. And I'm sure he does." Her stomach gave her another kick. He was very handsome. But untouchable. She dropped her gaze, smiled, and straightened her dress. His eyes would be the death of her if she continued to look into them.

Chalanor opened the door and stood aside so she could walk in. But she did not get very far. There on a rug in front of the open fire was her Prescott, almost naked making love to her best friend Bella. She didn't move. She watched with horror but also with fascination. The glow of the fire on their damp and heated bodies. She just stared at them. Then pulse speeding, heart beat pounding, heat flashed through her and she wanted to scream.

"Come away," Chalanor whispered. He took her gently by the arm.

She shook him off.

"No." Her head was buzzing. He had come to her and offered marriage after all. And she had accepted his proposal. Why was he doing this? My God, why? "Explain yourself, Prescott?" Her voice quivered as it rose. "Explain."

Prescott lifted his head and looked at her as his rush of release hit him. He began to laugh. Laugh out loud.

No. Her head was pounding. He had come to her and proposed marriage which she had accepted. Why was he doing this? Didn't he love her? My God, why?

Chalanor now had his hands on her upper arms trying to move her from the spot where she stood. But she fought him off again to no avail.

She turned her head to face him. "Leave me alone. No doubt you had a hand in this disgrace." She turned back and yelled at Prescott. "I want to know the meaning of this. Do you take me for a simpering simpleton?" She moved her hand to the right and slapped Chalanor in the chest. He did not flinch. "Get out of my way."

Chalanor dropped his arms and said nothing. But he did not leave. And he did not move. He probably wanted to enjoy her embarrassment and disgrace. Despite her churning stomach she was not only disgusted but furious. She would not swoon or cry as others might. She wanted an explanation. She would demand it.

Prescott was doing up his trousers and Bella started crying, while she looked for her clothes. She whimpered that she was sorry. "So very sorry."

"Tell me now. Why have you done this?" She was yelling but she did not care. Her pride was already wounded.

"I thought that was obvious, my dear." He continued to straighten his clothes.

"Obvious? No, it is not obvious. You could have asked her to marry you instead of me."

"Marry you? Marry her? I don't want either of you."

The sobs from Bella turned into cries of anguish. "You said you loved me, that's why I gave myself to you. You said it was me you wanted to marry. I'm ruined." She wept. Bella grabbed his arm and he pushed her to the floor. Her sobbing grew louder.

Louisa could hear voices and footsteps of others coming down the corridor. Soon everyone would know of Bella's fall and she felt sorry for her friend.

"You are nothing, either of you." Prescott continued. "I want neither of you. You are both harlots, ready to give yourself to any man. I have enjoyed both of you and now I am done."

"What nonsense is this? You're mad. I wouldn't give myself to you, ever." But her cries were useless as other people from the house party entered through the doors of the library behind her to witness the shame that lay before them. But she had not expected the performance she was now witnessing.

Prescott came to stand before her as he placed his shirt around himself.

"But I have had you. Just as you are a product of such a

dalliance. I am happy to soil your virtue, your non existing virtue." He was not looking at her but at the gathering audience. "She," he pointed at Bella, "was a dalliance, as are you." Now he pointed at her.

Bella screamed she was no dalliance but that Prescott loved her.

Louisa crossed her arms and stared at him. "You are nothing but a beast and I despise you."

"Thank you, my love." And he stormed from the room.

Louisa stood there her arms dropping to her side, unable to say anything or move from where she stood. She began to shake. Was it cold? She couldn't tell. He legs began to give way beneath her. This had to be some ridiculous dream. Her father was standing before her, looking into her eyes.

"My dear, come away."

"Father, what did he mean?"

She heard Chalanor's voice in the distance. "Take her away. Take her home. I will deal with this." She heard the tap of his boots as he left the room. The din around her closed in. She was so alone. Prescott was crazy but because he was aristocracy, they would believe him.

Her father turned her to the door and tried to get her through the crowd that had gathered. She heard comments but could not place from whose mouths they came. Their whispers penetrated her thoughts.

"Did you hear what he said? That he had had both of them."

"They are fallen women."

"They must have known he was a rake?"

"She will never be accepted into polite society ever again."

"After all she is but a bastard. That is what he said."

Louisa heard them but Prescott's comment that she was but a product of a dalliance went around and around in her head. A bastard. She looked around her. Each word, each movement and all the reactions she could see clearly. My God, what had he done? The things he said?

"Papa, what did he mean? I am no bastard? Am I?"

"Of course you aren't, my dear. Let us get you out of here." The noise of the crowd diminished as they made their way to her room.